DEMONHEART

Walkers From Another Dimension

J.J. EGOSI

CHAPTER 1
CALLS FROM A RESTLESS MIND

The air was cold. His footsteps echoed through the halls, each step pounding like a snapping avalanche against the floorboards. He felt a soreness in his mind, sensing he'd been taken far away from his realm of consciousness.

Michael had been walking down a darkened passageway for what seemed like an eternity. The wooden doors and gargoyle rings upon them ran with no end, slipping out from the shadows with each step he took. The halls were candlelit and ornamented with gothic paintings from times unknown to him. Empty suits of armor holding various forms of weaponry lined the walls, as if to protect them and what lied within.

This place intrigued and confused him. He had no recollection of how he got here, but was determined to find an answer.

At last, he approached the grand double doors at the end of the hall. He explored towards them with trembling legs. The doors were intricately decorated, with goat skulls on each handle and black wings on each side. Their crimson eyes pierced his mind, sending a shiver through his body.

As he prepared to knock and face whatever awaited him, the doors opened on their own. The creaking, with every painful inch they opened, left his heart thundering with dread.

He prepared himself to knock and face whatever awaited him beyond the doors. Not even the deep breath he took could help calm his speeding heart. He inched towards the doors when they opened on their own, creaking with every painful inch they moved.

A grand reading chamber revealed itself behind the doors. All the shelves were stacked with books to the ceilings. A fire sparked in the corner. The walls were clad in tapestries depicting a man and another: the shadow of a young girl. In the center of the chamber was the very man depicted in the tapestries.

This man appeared familiar to Michael. He sat on his scarlet leather-bound sofa, flipping through pages of a book as he held a glass of crimson wine in one hand. He took in the earthy scent with a mischievous grin running across his face.

The man's attire was somewhat formal: black dress shoes and pants, and a black shirt with the top two buttons undone. What was most peculiar, however, was the crow mask covering the top half of his face.

Michael's eyes were unwavering as they gazed at him. He did not know why he felt he had met him before, but the sensation was even more alluring.

Suddenly, the man closed the book and placed it onto the table beside him, before gazing in Michael's direction.

Michael stumbled back, feeling a sharp pain course through his body. He panted heavily in the man's presence, still unable to veer his attention from the faint crimson gaze through the crow mask.

The man leaned towards the chessboard laid across the table in front of him and picked up the king piece. He took one more sip of his wine before putting the glass down, twiddling the king piece between his fingers.

"So, it appears the stars have finally aligned for us, Michael." The man grinned under his crow mask, bringing a chill to the room.

"Who are you, and how do you know my name?" Michael exclaimed with sweat beading down his neck. "And your voice —it sounds so familiar."

He had a faint recollection of such a tone haunting his mind before fading away in the embers of the man before him.

The man smiled and stood up, then slowly walked towards Michael. Every step he took echoed while Michael's heart continued to pound. The man came to a few feet from him, stopped, and looked into Michael's eyes. "My name is Lucifer. Nice to finally meet you."

Michael's eyes widened. "Lucifer ... that name ..."—

"Sounds familiar, does it?" Lucifer interrupted. Michael took a step back from Lucifer, but the masked man persisted.

"It's him." What Isabella had told him about Hecate's master rang through his mind. In particular, the name she told him. He could recall nearly every bit of his encounter with the witch. Every word of hers and act of jealousy that led to a death he was grateful he did not have to witness. All the while, he could only imagine the person behind her maddening resolve. Until now.

The demon king.

Michael ran for an exit. The doors shut before he could reach them, closing them both in.

"Trying to leave so soon? Such poor manners, my friend."

"Let me go. You can't keep me captive!" Michael demanded.

"I think you'll be quite surprised by what I can and won't do." Lucifer grinned as a clap of lightning pierced through the sky. "I'm afraid escape is no longer an option. You're in my palace now. And in my palace, I have full control."

Michael shuddered both at the sight of the rain pouring down on the night and the flashing glow of a few bolts it cast on his grin as the rain bucketed down the windows. "What do you want from me? And why did you bring me here?"

Lucifer looked at him with intrigue. "I don't want much. Just a little conversation. And it was your own heart that led you here tonight, Michael."

"What are you talking about? I've never seen you or this palace before. I wouldn't even know how to get here if I wanted to," Michael refuted.

"Are you sure?" Lucifer asked. "Something tells me your mind carries more than your words are leading on."

Michael froze with fear. It was as if Lucifer had somehow penetrated his thoughts. The archangel knew of his name and where he learned it. Though he had a vague understanding of the threat he posed, the certainty that he had encountered him before petrified him most. Details of when and for why had escaped him. He could only question the demon king's reason for pursuing him even more.

He looked into the darkened red through the eyeholes in Lucifer's mask. Gritting his teeth, he refused to give him the satisfaction.

"You're full of shit," Michael exclaimed. "I'm sure it was you who brought me here. Now, tell me what you want."

Lucifer chuckled. "Oh, how defensive you've become. And rather naughty."

"Don't act as if you know me," Michael exclaimed.

"Perhaps I do. Would that be so wrong?" Lucifer asked. "More importantly, perhaps you also know me?"

Michael's lips quivered, leaving him standing in silence. His mind flooded with questions he feared having answered.

"To think you can only enter places based on trivial restraints such as locations and directions. You'll find one way or another that the most intriguing places are those you enter without finding at all." Lucifer looked out of his window with a curious grin.

"What the hell does any of that mean?" Michael asked with panic in his voice.

Lucifer frowned. "It appears you've lost sight of your old ways. What a pity. I was hoping we could have a more productive conversation tonight, but it seems you'll just have to stay here forever."

"What?" Michael shouted in a frantic rage. He searched for an exit in every direction, but all doors and windows were shut. He felt a tethering sensation around his ankles. What exactly, he could not see, but it left him petrified. Trapped. Forced to indulge in the demon king's words.

"You still don't get it, do you, Michael?" Lucifer took a deep breath and picked up his glass of wine. "You're in a dream right now."

"I'm dreaming?" Michael's heart sank to the bottom of his chest. A sense of confusion quickly swelled within.

"Yes, and a powerful dreamer you are, it seems," said Lucifer

"I am?" Michael wondered. "What does that mean?"

Lucifer took a sip of wine from his glass and looked at Michael with a smile. "When you have a dream, do you normally recall people or events from your reality?"

Michael thought back to all his past dreams of slaying orcs and dragons, recalling even the most minor detail.

"Most people forget them the instant they wake up. But I have a feeling you remember them clear as day," Lucifer replied. "In fact, I'm sure they feel so real to you. So frightening. So inescapable, just like right now."

Michael shivered at his words. Cold air filled the room at that moment, but the window remained closed and Lucifer's smile never left his face.

"The *Michael* in your dreams is the *Michael* that you believe to be the true you while you're dreaming. Is it not?"

"Isn't that what a dream is?" Michael's eyes widened with a terrifying realization that left him in silence for a moment. "Hold on. How do you even know what my dreams are about? There's no way you could have"—

"You have a lot to learn about me, Michael," Lucifer replied. "Let's first talk about why you think you're here. More importantly, I'd like to hear your explanation for how you can remember your reality outside of this dream. After all, it's strange to think about those outside of your dreams, isn't it? Most dreamers are engulfed in their temporary reality, yet all you can think of is what awaits you once you wake up."

Is it strange? Michael thought. *And what is he trying to get out of this conversation? I expected him to be far more brutish and commanding. Instead, he's so outlandish and buried in secrecy. Which feels even worse, somehow.*

"I don't know why I'm here," he spoke. "And I'm not sure how I can remember my life outside of this dream. Isabella. Julianna. And everything outside these walls. Usually, I'm a completely different *me* living a completely different life in a completely different world in my dreams. Now"—

"So, you do feel as if you never really left your reality behind, is that right?" asked Lucifer. "That perhaps those two are just behind those doors?

"Are they?" Michael darted his gaze towards the doors. Eerie darkness seeping from the goat eyes forced his attention towards Lucifer again. He could feel his body turn against its will as he clenched his jaws—fighting back.

"Just what is this spell you keep using?"

Lucifer smiled, showing little interest in his inquiry. He took a sip of wine and leaned back in his seat. "Let me ask you something. Have you ever felt pleasure or pain in your dreams?"

Michael looked into Lucifer's crimson eyes peering through the mask. They glowed, as if with amusement.

"What are you getting at?"

"In dreams, one cannot embrace the sensation of touch. You may be afraid of being burned alive by a ferocious dragon or bludgeoned by a horde of orcs, but that dragon's fire will never penetrate your senses. Neither will the clubs of orcs. Rather, you would simply wake up before the dragon ends you. That's because the death you experienced in your dream sent you back to your reality," said Lucifer.

"Are you saying dreams act as a backup form of living?" said Michael.

"I suppose you can think of it that way," Lucifer said with a laugh, handing Michael a full glass of wine.

Michael took the glass with reluctance. He held it and stared down at the wine's deep shade of red, seeing his crimson reflection.

"Tell me what you see in that glass, Michael," said Lucifer.

"I see my face," Michael replied.

"Yes, and that face is yours. I'm fairly certain you take on other personas in your other dreams. Now, tell me what you feel?" said Lucifer.

Michael's eyes widened, sensing the smooth material sliding from his fingertips and shattering onto the floor

"The glass! I could feel it!"

"Now, we're getting somewhere," Lucifer replied. "Damn shame you had to break my precious glass and put my premium wine to waste like that."

"Sorry, I'll clean it up," Michael said, frantically picking up the pieces.

"Don't worry about it," said Lucifer. "Besides, our business here is far from over."

With a snap of his fingers, the scattered pieces reformed into the wineglass, filling itself back with the spilled wine and placing itself on the table beside him.

Michael's eyes widened. "How did you do that?"

"Oh, you mean the reversal and alteration of time? I think the terminology speaks for itself. I went back in time to before the glass shattered and altered it, so it would still be where it was before I handed it to you," Lucifer replied.

"You can do that?" Michael asked.

"That, I can," Lucifer said with a grin. "Furthermore, I made it so neither of us would forget any part of our conversation. Perhaps you remember a thing or two you didn't know a few seconds prior."

Michael's eyes widened with fear as the surrounding walls closed in under Lucifer's haunting smile.

He's a complete lunatic! he thought. *What kind of power is this?*

"My power is unmatched, Michael. It's unlike anything you've seen before. And as for calling me a lunatic; I'm hurt. I thought we were finally getting to know each other," said Lucifer.

"How were you able to"—Michael demanded.

"Able to what? Read your mind? I told you. My power is unmatched," said Lucifer.

Michael stepped back, shaking. "Get away from me right now!"

"Or what? You'll kill yourself in this dream, bringing you back to your reality? It doesn't take a mind reader to know what you're planning. Your face says it all," said Lucifer, grinning.

"Jus: leave me alone!" Michael stumbled. Lucifer followed him with his head spited, tilted with intrigue.

"You know, many of the most powerful dreamers over the eons have gained an awareness of dreams and have taken advantage of their gift. Many start acting recklessly, stealing from the poor, raping all the women in sight, and killing anyone who gets in their way. Money, sex, and power are what drive one's soul, Michael."

Michael envisioned such a world, certain it already existed. A world he refused to be a part of.

"And with no consequences to dictate one's dreams, the soul's most blasphemous desires are acted out in the fullest. Without shame or hesitation. This is an undeniable truth that dreams flesh out for me to see."

The images continued to eat at his mind. He saw himself plunging into the same horrid reality with the memories of his alcohol addiction.

Lucifer watched with amusement the sweat bead down Michael's face.

"Perhaps you're already showing symptoms. Julianna and Isabella were their names, correct? I hope you're treating them well. After all, they offered you such compassion when the rest of the world tossed you to the fucking dogs!"

Michael's blood boiled at the very notion. The longer he let the thought infiltrate his mind, the sooner he saw himself becoming the nightmare Lucifer had painted.

"Jus: shut up. I'm nothing like that," Michael demanded.

"Is that a fact?" Lucifer chuckled.

"Yes!" Michael insisted. "As for Julianna and Isabella, I'd never lay a finger on them."

"Oh?"

"Because you're right." Tears spilled down from the tender memories he shared with them. From his childhood days with Isabella to the moment they reconciled. To the growing happiness he felt with Julianna through their journey capturing the elementals, and now as the three of them formed a kinship as one.

"I've stricken a rather delightful chord, haven't I?" Lucifer asked. "Many people who gain such power go mad with it, Michael—carrying out their wildest fantasies in their realities, leaving them broken and dead in the end."

"I already told you I don't fit that description," Michael refuted. "I have no interest. Only in"—

"Maintaining the friendships you've finally earned for yourself," Lucifer interjected.

Michael's heart skipped a beat. He felt both his mind and soul being read through the darkening slits of Lucifer's mask. His heinous grin tore at Michael's seams.

"Power comes in many forms, Michael ... and it all comes from the same place. Desire."

Lucifer leaned forward. He snickered as the nose of his mask brushed against Michael's trembling face.

"You desire to be heard. To be recognized and accepted by those around you."

"Stop it." Michael's breathing got heavy. The miasma he sensed before thickened. It gripped at his fledgling mind. "Just back off."

"Here's another thing to consider," Lucifer said. "Power also comes from fear. And what you fear is to be forgotten—to be cast aside."

"Enough," Michael pleaded. He saw the images of Isabella and Julianna washing away. His memories of them together fading.

"I wonder how you'll turn out," Lucifer began. "Will you be cast aside like the pariah you've always been or will you let your own need for fitting into this world destroy what you have?"

"You're fucking psychotic." Michael's eyes flared with

contempt. "Just get me out of here already! This conversation is over!"

Lucifer grabbed Michael by the front of his shirt and slammed him against the wall. His heart raced from the sudden aggression and the usual calmness Lucifer still possessed as he gripped him.

"Not until you tell me why you think you're here!"

The fear in Michael's eyes grew to a point where he broke into tears again. "I don't know. I just want to go back to my friends so I can help them on our mission."

"Mission, you say?" Lucifer grinned, loosening his grip.

"Yes, the three of us want to stop the Legion of Morningstar from destroying the world with the titan rings," said Michael, calming down.

"Really? That seems ambitious. Wouldn't you say?" Said Lucifer. "After all, you must be aware by now I'm the driving force of your opposition."

"Maybe. So, what?" Michael's eyes widened.

"You still don't get it?" asked Lucifer.

"Get what?" said Michael, growing flustered.

"While you may have all agreed to defeat the Legion of Morningstar, is this really a promise you can uphold? A reasonable endeavor?"

"Are you threatening me now?" Michael demanded.

"Surely, you're aware of our intentions with the titan rings and the challenge that'll come with taking them from us. How exactly do you plan to do that? Will you hope to draw out our remaining members with the ring you took from Hecate? I'm afraid the rest of us can't be seduced so easily."

Lucifer leaned forward until Michael could feel his breath against his face. The hot air mixed with the aroma of wine left him shaking.

"Or perhaps you'll seek them all out yourself and take the rings for your nefarious desires. I've read that story all too many times and I know how it ends. What may just be bottled up thoughts you've been keeping for a while are potentially the reason you're here. A frail man mistreated by the world ... Seeking the power needed to reap revenge. A restless soul is the damnedest thing, isn't it? What a pity it must be to be you," said Lucifer with a grin.

"That's enough!" said Michael, shoving Lucifer back.

"I said nothing you didn't already know. Tell me; how do you plan on carrying out such an ambitious mission?" said Lucifer as he dusted himself off.

"I don't know. Julianna's a great fighter and Isabella's got a titan of her own now, plus that ax. And I" —

"So, you aim to lean on those two little demon girls to get the job done? I wonder if that plan of yours derives itself from oversight or insight. What do you last recall from before arriving here? Just curious," said Lucifer.

As if in a trance, Michael thought back to what he was doing before his dream. Another dream. One he'd never had before. "I recall something from another world crashing into mine and changing it forever."

"There's my answer," said Lucifer.

"There's what answer? What does my last memory even mean?" Michael asked.

"All will be made clear soon enough, my friend. Just stay patient and the bells of time will chime in a new era in your life," said Lucifer.

"Enough with the riddles!"

"You're no fun, Michael. If you wanted a straight answer, you should have just asked me for one," said Lucifer. He walked back to his chair, holding up the king piece behind his back. Michael reluctantly followed him.

At the snap of his fingers, another chair appeared across him. "Take a seat, Michael. You and I are about to play a game. To see if you really have a chance at defeating me. Perhaps one of us will be surprised in the end."

"But I don't even know this game," said Michael, already bewildered.

Lucifer replied, "You might know it better than you think. Try it. You just might surprise yourself."

Michael's exasperation dwindled as he focused on the game board in front of him. He laid a puzzled look at the two rows of white pieces on his side, facing the black pieces on the opposite side.

"This game is chess, right?"

Lucifer grinned. "Very good. And you realized that all on your own, having never seen this game in your life, correct?"

Michael's face grew pale from shock. *He's right! I've no recollection of ever playing or watching anyone play this game in my life, yet I knew it as if I did. How is this possible? Is this another one of his spells?*

"You're destined for great things, Michael. But I'm sure you already knew that," Lucifer said, moving his pawn piece forward.

Michael shook as he matched Lucifer's opening move. "There. That's my move."

"Well, that wasn't very inspiring, but it'll have to do," said Lucifer

"What is that supposed to mean? It's the same move you made," Michael argued.

"Exactly. Innovation will grant you victory, but copying the moves of your adversaries will lead to a quick defeat. Is that what you want?"

"Just make your move." Michael gritted his teeth.

"Are you hiding your knowledge for the game behind that mediocre move because you wish to prove all my words wrong somehow, or is it because you hope to end this game quickly with my victory, getting you back to the life you so desire?" Lucifer asked.

Michael's entire body quivered as his breathing grew heavier.

"My turn." With a grin, Lucifer moved his pawn piece forward.

Michael nodded and then mirrored his move.

"A wise man strives for innovation on the battlefield. Mimicry, however, is for fools." Lucifer made his next move: sliding the king piece forward.

"The king? But why would you move your best piece out in the open like that?" Michael asked.

Lucifer grinned. "There's the chess master I know. And to answer your question, a great king leads his men from the front lines of battle, Michael."

He keeps acting as if he knows me, and yet no matter how hard I try, I can't seem to remember ever meeting you, Michael thought as he moved his knight piece. *But what if he actually knows me and I know him?*

He recalled his encounter with Hecate again and the way she spoke of the demon king's demands. Specifically for him. Paired with the sense of familiarity he still carried, the unease of another potentially lost memory worsened.

"Some memories are more difficult to dig up than others." Lucifer moved his king piece forward again.

Lucifer's words startled Michael.

"Did I frighten you?" Lucifer asked. "Or did you remember something truly chilling about yourself?"

"Quiet." Michael gritted his teeth. To shake off the frustration, he glanced at the chessboard and the peculiar move Lucifer had made.

"That strategy has a major flaw, don't you think?" Michael focused on moving his pawn pieces forward as a few turns passed.

"I have no idea what you're talking about," said Lucifer with sarcasm, as he moved his pawn pieces forward as well.

"So much for not copying moves," said Michael.

"My moves are nothing like yours. Not when I still lead with my king and you sacrifice your pawns for an early game advantage." Lucifer grinned, taking Michael's third pawn piece in a row.

"A true player of the game knows his pawns are just as valuable as any of his other pieces. I know you're aware of this, so how about you stop holding back?" Lucifer said, capturing Michael's fourth pawn piece.

Michael took a deep breath and did as Lucifer requested. He moved the pieces at the back forward, and Lucifer copied him, while still leading with his king piece. The two of them started capturing each other's pieces, one by one, until half the game's pieces on each side were captured.

Michael moved his queen piece out into the open field. Lucifer raised his eyebrow. "You wish to place your queen in such a compromising position?"

"Yes, I do. I believe in my queen. As the king's right hand, she'll lead me to victory by ensnaring your army and leaving your king defenseless," said Michael.

"The queen? A king's right hand?" Lucifer turned towards the single painting of a silhouette depicting a young girl. He sneered, then shook his head before turning towards Michael. "Not if I block with my castles and bishops."

Michael captured a series of Lucifer's pieces, leaving him with the king piece alone. His confidence grew as he cornered Lucifer's king piece with his. Lucifer grinned.

"Oh, how the arrogant have fallen."

"What are you saying? You're the one without your strongest"—Michael started. He looked down at the board, realizing its current state.

"You say you believe in your queen, and yet where is she?" Lucifer asked.

Michael's eyes widened. "My queen"—He exclaimed in total disbelief.

"That's right. You were so busy chipping away at my army, you didn't even see me snatch your queen off the board. And with a pawn, of all pieces," said Lucifer.

"No, that can't be."

"Oh, yes, it can. And with only our kings left on the board, it leaves us at a stalemate. A state where neither of us can win nor lose," Lucifer said.

"A stalemate?" Michael looked at the almost empty board with a smirk. "It seems you don't care about your soldiers as much as you said."

"But I kept you from winning, did I not?" Lucifer asked. "And that, somehow, a victory. Because it means you didn't win, either."

"So, that was really your plan." Michael scowled.

"Indeed. It seems we're evenly matched. However, if you're looking for a change of fortune, I have another for you," said Lucifer. He pulled out a deck of cards from the drawer of the table beside him.

"A card game?"

"Yes, and I'd like for you to do the honor of shuffling. Do so well. I'd hate for you to be dealt a bad hand. Or another bad hand, I suppose." Lucifer grinned.

"Fine, I will! I don't trust you, anyway." Michael said, shuffling his deck and placing it on the table.

"Here's how the game works. To settle who wins the chess game, we will each draw one card from the top of the deck. Whoever draws the higher card wins," said Lucifer.

The pace of Michael's heartbeat increased with suspense.

"Feeling nervous, are we?" Lucifer began. "Would you prefer I go first? Maybe that'll ease the tension."

"Fine, you go first," said Michael.

"With pleasure." Lucifer revealed the top card of his deck to be the king of hearts.

Michael's eyes widened. "No way! You drew a king!"

"I told you we're evenly matched. If you want to beat me, you'll have to draw something quite impressive from the deck," said Lucifer.

Letting him go first didn't help at all, Michael thought, *And I'm not even sure I know how to play this game ... Or do I? Just what the hell is going on? Where are these memories coming from?*

"I'm waiting, Michael," Lucifer said.

Michael bit back his confusion and fear. *That's not the point! I can figure this all out once I get back to my friend. That's all I really care about. Not beating this masked lunatic. I just want to get out of this nightmare already!*

Lucifer frowned. "Are you going to draw a card or not? I'm growing bored."

"Very well." Michael's hand inched towards the deck, struggling to pick among the stack until he picked one at random in the center. He trembled as he pulled out the card and slowly turned it towards himself, revealing it as the ace of spades. He looked at his card with outrage. Lucifer grinned.

"No It's a *one*. That's the lowest card in the deck."

Lucifer chuckled. "Quite the contrary. The ace is an incredibly diverse card in that it can either act as the lowest card or the highest card, depending on the outcome you desire," said Lucifer.

"Depending on the outcome I desire?" Michael asked.

"Yes, your destiny is in your hands. You can call a victory right now by calling your ace a high card, defeating my king, or you can call it a low card, handing me the victory instead. You drew the card, so only you can decide. Will you choose to defeat my king of hearts or will you choose to see what awaits you behind the door of defeat?" asked Lucifer.

Michael's heart raced with anxiety. Panting heavily, he looked down at the card and back up at Lucifer. "I call neither."

Lucifer grinned. "Neither, you say? Does that mean?"—

"Yes," Michael said, cutting Lucifer off. "You said my destiny is in my hands. Well, I'll decide how this game will end when I'm good and ready. For now, I have more questions to answer. How could I be the archangel? Who is the Legion of Morningstar? And what are the dimension titans really all about? It's too early to win or lose when I don't even know what's on the line."

"How right you are. I think we're finally done here," said Lucifer.

"You mean?"—said Michael with surprise as the doors behind him flung open.

"You and I will meet again soon. Until then, protect your new pieces and grab your victory before someone else does," said Lucifer.

"My new pieces?"

SUDDENLY, MICHAEL WOKE UP IN HIS TENT. HE frantically scanned his surroundings, covered in sweat.

"I'm back?" He took a sigh of relief, recognizing the piles of clothing and liquor bottles laid across the floor of his tent.

He quickly threw on some clothes and stumbled outside. The surroundings of their new campsite were a lush and open field surrounded by a ring of trees in the distance, spread in the very center of the Twilight Forest.

"Yes. It's all coming back."

In his moment of a very vivid and foreboding dream, he nearly forgot the discussion he had with Julianna and Isabella a few days prior.

"Why are we leaving the outskirts again?" Michael asked.

The three of them hiked their way out of the Light Realm with all their belongings, bound for where both the realm of Light and Dark touched.

"I told you last night, or did you forget?" Julianna said.

"Sorry. Mind telling me again?" Michael asked with a nervous smile.

Julianna sighed. "We can't be seen by either of the two major surrounding kingdoms. Two demons and an angel, I mean."

"That would be a problem for a lot of reasons," Michael replied.

"Yes, between the light realm that hates demons and the dark realm that hates ... well ... you." Isabella began.

"Thanks," Michael said with a dim eyed look.

"It just isn't safe," Isabella said.

"Will you two be alright? Leaving your homes, that is. And your businesses. I don't wish to be a burden," Michael looked down with a downhearted stare.

"You're not a burden. We'll be fine as long as we're careful," Isabella answered.

"Besides, an assassin can run her business anywhere," Julianna said.

"I should be fine, too," Isabella added.

"If you say so," Michael replied. "Twilight Forest, it is."

"And days of intense training, here we come," Julianna stated.

Michael nodded as she stood in Twilight Forest, remembering with half a smile the discussion.

They care a great deal about me. Enough to leave their homes behind and join me, he thought.

Michael watched Isabella and Julianna train just as they had planned. Isabella practiced with the new ax she claimed from Hecate, while Julianna practiced new dual-wielding strategies.

Those two are fighting rather early in the morning, he thought.

He approached them to get a closer look, then stopped.

Wait, he thought. *That was just a dream, but I know that was really him: the demon king, Lucifer. The guy we're after. I need to inform them of this fast.*

With a confident breath, he stomped forward with his hands balled. Meanwhile, the girls battled with grins of exhilaration on their faces, moving swiftly through the wind as their weapons sliced the air.

"You're not half bad for a jewelry heiress." Julianna smiled, slashing at Isabella's ax with her swords, one after the other at a ferocious pace.

"Don't act all surprised." Isabella quickly locked both her swords in place with the edge of her ax, staring back with a smile. "All aristocrats are taught the art of weapon-wielding at a young age. Though I have no fighting experience aside from my plight with Hecate, you'll find I'm a fast learner."

Julianna smirked. "Don't get cocky. I murder for a living and these swords have shed a great deal of blood."

She pulled both her swords out of the hold of Isabella's ax, slashing them in a single movement like a wave of gleaming iron under the sun.

"Is that a threat?" Isabella grinned.

"Perhaps it is." Julianna grinned back. "You'll have to fight a lot better if you want to win Michael's heart."

"No problem," Isabella refuted.

The two of them continued to spar, sending sparks against one another's blades when they noticed Michael approaching.

"Speak of the angel," Julianna said.

"I thought you were going to give me lessons in duel-wielding," said Michael as he walked over to them.

"So, you finally woke up, I see. It's almost noon, you know?" said Julianna.

"Sorry, I had this really weird dream," said Michael.

"You tell us that every day," said Isabella.

"Yeah, I guess I do," said Michael. He paused and thought back to his dreams over the past couple of weeks.

"Anyway, I'm busy getting Isabella in shape. Between her lack of familiarity with her new weapon and her weak healing magic, she'll be easy to beat," said Julianna.

"Oh, fuck off! You know it was my healing magic that won me my battle against Hecate," said Isabella.

"That and your new *etherial* form," Julianna began, "I still can't believe you could achieve such power. I must admit I'm a bit jealous."

"Remember that the next time you try talking down to me," Isabella replied.

"As for you, Michael, I told you we'd be sparring this morning at seven. Would it kill to get up in time?"

Michael remembered the last two training sessions he spent with her, both of which ended in his quick defeat; his sword was tossed through the air and he fell against the ground back first and aching before rising to repeat the same experience against his better judgment until the sunset.

"Actually, it just might."

Julianna groaned. "Your lack of resolution is your problem. You grew up a servant, so you never felt you could achieve much. Well, that changes now, do you understand?"

Michael took a deep breath, recalling his encounter with Lucifer. Every second left him chilling with despair but also filled him with the resolution she spoke of. To change his destiny for himself.

"I understand," Michael began. "And there's something I'd like to tell you. Both of you, actually."

"Really?" Julianna asked.

"Must be pretty serious for you to be wearing that stoic face," Isabella said.

The two of them snickered in amusement, as Michael took a deep breath, ready to unfurl the findings in his dream.

Suddenly, the sky warped, changing colors into a distorted grid-like appearance. It was like nothing they'd ever seen before, stopping them all in place as something tore its way through.

"What's going on?" Isabella asked.

"My vision. Of something from another world," said Michael. "It's just like what I saw in my dream with him. But what is it? What does it mean?"

"Your what?" Julianna asked, confused.

The cacophony brought by the fissure forming in the sky blocked out their conversation. They watched in awe as a strange golden aircraft plummeted like a meteor towards the ground. Its impact created a massive crater.

Lost for words, Michael and the girls cautiously approached this otherworldly phenomenon. A sinking dread consumed him, certain that what laid before him did, in fact, come from another world.

CHAPTER 2
UNEXPECTED VISITORS

None of them had ever seen anything like this before—the sky tearing apart. A strange object plummeting down in a bit of smoke and quaking the ground was all as strange as it was unsettling to them.

Julianna slowly approached the crater as it filled with steam from the unidentified object.

"What do you think this thing is?"

"I have no idea. I've never seen anything like it before," said a bewildered Isabella.

"I think that Hecate woman may have been telling the truth about the existence of multiple dimensions," Julianna replied, her eyes fixated on the clearing steam emitting from the object to reveal its golden shade.

"You think this thing came from another dimension?" Isabella asked.

"I do. As for which dimension, I suppose we'll find out soon enough," said Julianna.

"Dimensions?" Michael thought. *"Other worlds?"*

He gulped, startled by the touch of Isabella's hand on his shoulder.

"Whatever you were telling us before, I think it'll have to wait."

Michael lost himself in bewilderment. He nodded with hesitation. "But, can it?"

The three of them watched in amusement as the entire golden aircraft came into view, revealing its disheveled state.

Suddenly, the doors on either side of the object opened before two figures made their way out. The figures came in the clear—enough to be apparent as women. One of them had jagged chin-length blue hair, and the other had straight elbow-length pink hair, each covering their forehead with bangs. They took a proper gander at Michael and his friends, who responded with unnerved looks.

"Unreal. There were people in that thing?" Michael said.

"Yeah, people..." Said Julianna.

Her response completely flew over Michael. "What's that supposed to mean?"

"Women are just fucking falling from the sky to be with you, aren't they?" Isabella pouted.

"Well, I don't know about that..." Michael replied with a nervous laugh.

The two women dusted themselves off and then climbed out of the crater to the same level of ground as he and his friends. The woman with pink hair darted towards Michael and stopped a few inches from him.

"Hey, haven't you ever heard of personal space?" Isabella shouted.

"Calculating," the woman instead replied with an unusual device in her hand.

"Excuse me. When someone talks to you, the decent thing to do is make some damn eye contact," Isabella said, growing more annoyed.

"I don't think she's listening," said Julianna.

"Is there anything we can help you with?" Michael nervously asked.

He inspected the woman. She had on a pair of black leather boots, pants to complement the dark theme her low-cut top also embraced, and a black trench coat. He'd never seen anyone dress like that before. Still, he could tell by her crimson gaze she was a demon.

"Calculating," the pink-haired woman repeated.

The blue-haired woman moved around Julianna and Isabella, sniffing them like an animal. She was also clad in all black—flatter shoes, shorts, a low-cut top, but no trench coat. Her eyes were a deep shade of red to the other woman's.

They're both demons? Michael thought. *Just where did they come from?*

"Hey, what do you think this is, you freak?" Julianna said to the blue-haired woman.

"Yeah, if this is your way of communicating, you're just as much of your weirdo as your friend over there," Isabella said, now frustrated with both of them.

"Done calculating. This man doesn't have what we're looking for. He's useless," said the pink-haired woman, looking in Michael's eyes with daggers.

"Hey, who are you calling useless?" Michael said, annoyed.

"I am calling *you* useless. You do not have what I am looking for. Must I repeat myself?"

"What a piece of work this woman is." Isabella scowled.

Julianna whispered, "Hey, look at their eyes. They must be demons like us."

"And potentially dangerous," Isabella replied, almost losing herself in their gazes.

"They could be working with the Legion of Morningstar," Julianna said.

That's right, Michael thought as he gazed at the entity from which they crawled out. *They very well could.*

The pink-haired woman looked them all in the eye with suspicion before looking at her travel companion. "Have you found anything over there?"

"Not yet, but this girl with the orange hair gives off a strange scent," said the blue-haired girl.

"Really?" the pink-haired girl said, raising her eyebrow. She walked up to Isabella, pointing her device at her.

"Hey, are you two just going to ignore us? We want answers!" Julianna demanded. "Just what are you doing here?"

The pink-haired woman looked over at Julianna before scanning Isabella. "We want answers, as well. If you have what we're looking for, perhaps we can entertain your trivial demands," said the pink-haired girl.

"Trivial?" Julianna's face reddened.

What is it they're looking for? Michael thought to himself. His eyes then widened. A realization sunk deep into his mind.

Suddenly, the pink-haired girl's device beeped out of control. "Yes, this girl has what we came for."

"What are you talking about?" Isabella asked.

The pink-haired girl put her device in her pocket and pointed at Isabella, catching her off guard.

"Hand over the dimension titan now."

"Like hell, I will!" Isabella shouted. "First you just crashed from nowhere and completely ignored us when we talked to you. Now you think you can just steal from us? Seriously? How about you start by telling us where the hell you came from? You fucking creeps don't even know our names and you're getting in our faces, smelling and scanning with your weird golden device."

"You want pleasantries and their tedious qualities? Fine." The pink-haired woman sighed. "Very well, my name is Alexa and I come from the sixth dimension."

The sixth? Isabella thought as she recalled Hecate's chant before summoning her titan. *She's not from the same world as her, then.*

"My partner, if you could call her that, comes from the first dimension." Alexa continued, "Her name is unimportant."

"Well, I think they'd like to know what it is." She turned away from Alexa. "My name is Ursula. Super nice to meet you guys, by the way," the blue-haired girl said, whiffling hands with Michael and his friends.

"A pleasure meeting you," Michael said as he shook her hand. His feeling of unease deepened. *What exactly are other dimensions like?*

"Do you come from other planets?" Isabella asked.

"No, same planet." Ursula smiled. "Just different time periods "

Alexa sighed. "Yes, very nice. Make friends with the natives. You do realize that will only make killing them off more difficult for you, right?" Alexa interjected. She covered the top half of her face with her hand, embarrassed.

"Wait, you're going to kill us?" Michael asked in astonishment.

"Possibly. However, you might get lucky if you hand over the ring and choose your words wisely when explaining exactly how you attained it," Alexa said. "I wouldn't count on it, though. The people who carry these rings tend to be of the malevolent persuasion."

"Bold words coming from someone who wants it," Isabella said, coldly.

"Even bolder coming from the one keeping it to herself," Alexa snapped.

"Why don't you just cut the shit and tell us why you want the rings and maybe you'll be the lucky ones," Julianna said.

"Happy to." Alexa smiled. "Ursula and I are dimension

walkers. We scour all corners of the omniverse for its greatest treasures."

"And in this case, you're after the titan rings?" Michael asked with a stern gaze.

Tension filled both him and his friends as the severity of the visitors' intentions sank in.

"Yes. You'll be impressed to know we currently have three titans," said Alexa.

"Are you serious? You already possess three out of the seven titan rings?" Michael's head spun with fear.

"Yeah, and our adversary only has two," Ursula interjected.

"You weren't supposed to say that, dumbass," Alexa shouted.

"Sorry," Ursula whimpered.

"Your adversary?" Michael's eyes widened.

Alexa sighed, and then continued, "That's right. As my bumbling partner said, they're trailing us by just one titan."

"So, you're racing for influence is what you're saying?" Julianna suggested.

"Correct. And the first person to claim four titans will be the winner of the race," Alexa said.

"Because that would mean no one can have more than you. Not your adversary. No one." Julianna nodded with a better understanding.

"I like the sound of that. You come off as a woman of business, which I can respect," Said Isabella.

Alexa grinned. "I am. I own Clockwork Designs, the largest military base in the entire omniverse. No one designs more hi-tech or devastating weaponry than I do, and no one ever will."

Impressed, Julianna said, "You're quite confident. What sorts of weapons do you make?"

"I make many types: missiles, cannons, rockets, tanks...

the list goes on. I also lead countless soldiers, the world over," said Alexa.

"Sounds like you're the queen or something to have that kind of power," Isabella joked.

"I am," Alexa said with a proud grin.

Isabella and Julianna looked at her in stunned silence.

"I hope my title of the sixth dimension's queen makes it clear to you three that I get what I want. Without fail."

"Hold on," Michael began. "Are we just going to ignore the part where they told us about their search for the titan rings?"

"Right," Ursula began with a friendly smile. "So what Alexa was saying was that we're actually doing the omniverse a service by collecting these titans."

"Are you now?" Julianna raised an eyebrow.

"Yeah." Ursula nodded. "Our enemy's led by this super bad guy that wants to use them to take over the omniverse, so the obvious option to stop him is to capture them all."

Julianna's eyes widened. "You speak of immense opposition. Do they go by a name?"

"Yes, the Legion of Morningstar," said Ursula.

Michael and his friends froze in place because of the revelation. They looked at her in stunned silence, completely dumbfounded.

Ursula looked around, confused. "What? Did I say something wrong?"

If their enemy is the same as ours, our goals could align, right? Michael thought. But he couldn't shake the bad feeling about them.

Alexa slapped her on the back of the head. "You weren't supposed to tell them who we're after, either. Now, they're going to want to go after them, as well."

"Sorry. I didn't know," Ursula said, rubbing the back of her head.

"You never know anything, you nitwit," Alexa yelled. "Just shut your mouth from now on."

"We already know about your secret. We're already acquainted with the Legion of Morningstar," said Julianna.

"In fact, I just killed off one of their members. That's how I got my titan," Isabella said, matter-of-factly.

Alexa scowled. She rushed towards her and grabbed the front of her shirt. "You mean to tell me you've encountered a member of their legion, defeated them, and took their ring?"

"Yes," said Isabella, struggling to breathe because of Alexa's grip.

Alexa put her down, then took a deep breath. "I see. When I heard the Legion's titan count went from three to two, I figured it was because one of them was stolen. I never would have thought someone from this glorified landfill of a dimension could defeat one of their members and take their ring, no less!"

"Well, I did. And I have this shiny new ax to prove it!" Isabella said with her chin raised as she pulled the ax from her infinity bag. She oozed with confidence and showoff.

Alexa's attitude irritated Michael. "Who are you calling a glorified landfill?" he asked.

"Believe me. It was a compliment. I swear this air is going to make me sick." Alexa coughed with disgust. Ursula did the same.

"Sure doesn't feel like one," Michael groaned.

Alexa looked back at him with a smug grin. The gleam of Isabella's blade caught her attention and shocked her.

"An unholy relic?" Alexa's eyes widened, and she smiled. "You are who you say you are. I am convinced of that now."

"Hey, where did you get that cool bag?" Ursula asked with intrigue.

"You like it? It's an infinity bag. Julianna made one for me.

Promise to leave us alone and I'm sure she'll make one for you, too." Isabella said with a smile.

Ursula's face lit up with joy.

"No promises..." said Julianna, looking the other way.

Alexa sighed. "Why would you want such an arcane piece of technology? You know my dimension has far more advanced equipment than some infinity bag."

"Hey, you seem to be pretty knowledgeable about stuff like the titan rings, the Legion of Morningstar, these unholy relics, and even these infinity bags," said Michael.

"And your point?" Alexa asked.

"My point is I'd like you to tell us what else you know. You see, the member of the Legion of Morningstar we killed told me that their leader is after me. Do you know him on a personal level?" Michael asked.

Julianna and Isabella signaled with their hands to stop him from saying any more, but it was too late.

"You're about as airheaded as Ursula. No, I don't know him personally. Nor do I even know his name. They say he works in secrecy," said Alexa.

That means I must wait until these two leave before I can reveal the details of my encounter. Or at least until I think I can trust them. He thought.

"However, I'm thinking we kidnap you and use you to draw their leader out. If one of their members said their leader is looking for you, in particular, then it must be true. No one from that organization just asks for someone by name," said Alexa.

"Hey, who do you think you are, threatening to take my boyfriend from me?" Julianna said, grabbing Michael by his arm.

"Boyfriend? That's my husband you're talking about!" said Isabella, grabbing onto his other arm.

"Is this really the best time?" Michael asked, aching from the tugging of his limbs on either side.

Alexa watched in astonished silence as they tugged at his arms. "I'm surrounded by morons."

"At least you've got me by your side," Ursula said with an eager smile.

Alexa's blood boiled, unable to bear everyone around her any longer. She panted heavily as the last of her restraint left her.

"Damn it. Don't speak until you're spoken to!"

Alexa hit Ursula across the face and knocked her to the floor. She kicked up the dirt from the grass under her feet with a thud.

Isabella and Julianna watched in shock. Michael broke from their grips and marched up to Alexa with disdain in his eyes.

"Hey, what the fuck was that for?" he yelled.

"She was being insubordinate," said Alexa. "And I don't tolerate that sort of behavior."

"Look, I don't understand half the shit you say, but I know that you don't just go around hitting people," Michael replied, gritting his teeth.

"How I treat this girl is none of your concern," Alexa replied, watching as tears rolled down Ursula's dirt-covered face.

"It is if I see it.," Michael insisted, grabbing Alexa by either collar of her trench coat.

Isabella and Julianna laid an unfleeting look at him as he stood up to Alexa. Ursula looked up from the ground, smiling with a whimper as she wiped her tears away. She dusted herself off and stood with restraint. She knew better than to react. Instead, she flashed a bloodied grin of submission.

Alexa looked down at Michael's trembling hands and scoffed at his remark before slapping them away. "You'll be taken captive no matter how I treat Ursula. I'm afraid you don't get a say in this."

Michael shook in presence of the woman Alexa just hit, and then a devious smirk formed across his face. "I suggest you change your tone unless you want to find out, firsthand, why the Legion's leader is seeking me out."

"Are you threatening me?" Alexa asked with a surprised smile.

"I don't make threats. I make promises. And I promise to teach you some manners right here and now unless you apologize to your friend," said Michael.

"She's not my friend!" Alexa shouted. "And I have no use for such things."

"Well, she's something if she traveled all the way here with you," Julianna insisted.

"She's the same thing you are." Alexa gritted her teeth. "... just disposable pieces of flesh. Waiting to be thrown to the slaughterhouse once they've reached their full use."

"You're sick!" Michael shouted.

"I'm giving you a dose of reality," said Alexa. "Those two girls over there? The ones who seem so infatuated with you? Do you think they'll be around forever? I doubt it."

"What are you saying?" Michael replied.

"Once they get what they want, be it sex or children or money, you'll be on the streets, just like Ursula was before I was gracious enough to pick her up."

Get what they want?

Memories of his encounter with Lucifer flooded in. He remembered the painfully awakening words Lucifer said about desires leaving a trail of ruin. His heart sunk when he imagined plunging back into a life of servitude with no escape.

"So, you'll excuse me when I tell you I know what's best

for Ursula," Alexa said, standing closer to Michael and looking him straight in his eyes.

"You don't scare me, Alexa," Michael said with a nervous gulp.

"Then, you haven't been paying attention," said Alexa.

She turned to Isabella. Her face somehow blended a friendly smile and a menacing stare. Her demon eyes fixated on Isabella's. Alexa took a graceful step toward her. Isabella grinned to mask her fear, but Alexa could see past it.

"Don't forget you still have something I want."

"I haven't," Isabella replied with a callous gaze.

"And when I take it, I'll be also taking your precious husband to bait out the Legion's leader," said Alexa.

"Not if I can help it!" Michael thundered.

His aura grew. The still wind heightened into a raging tempest. A tributary of cracks formed in the ground as it crumbled. Michael released his wings and summoned his scepter. His eyes turned into blue incandescence, looking piercingly at Alexa. He plastered a look of awe on everyone's face. His form left Alexa's eyes agape. It was almost as if she succumbed to fear.

"If the way you treat Ursula is any sign of how you treat people, then I won't allow you to lay a hand on Isabella. I don't know what you plan on doing with the titan rings once you have them. For all I know, you could be planning to use them for evil, as well. Either way, if you want to kidnap me, you'll have to defeat me first!" said Michael.

"So, this is his archangel form?" said an awestruck Julianna, feeling his divine presence take her breath away.

"It's even more beautiful than I remember," Isabella said.

"Is he?"

"He is," Alexa said to Ursula. "The prophecies are true. This man is the archangel, Michael."

"The prophecies?" Isabella asked.

"Yes I thought it was just a legend. I mean, it talks about a time we could never even conceptualize as our reality."

"Wait, I'm lost," said Ursula. "Are you saying Michael came from a time before our own?"

"We knew that much." Isabella turned towards Michael with a bewildering glare. Julianna did the same.

"But how long before our time?" Julianna asked.

"I'm afraid so," Alexa continued. "The prophecy talks of two primordial forces of light and dark that fought over the monotheistic rights to the omniverse. It was a battle spanning eons, as expected from two evenly matched deities. Neither could defeat the other so they slumbered in the outskirts of the world, only to be awoken by the return of the titans, so their rivalry can continue again."

Michael grew dizzy, overcome by the revelation. He questioned its legitimacy with fear as Lucifer's crow-masked face appeared in his mind.

"It seems the time is now. Michael, you're that force of light. Its safe to assume the leader of the Legion of Morningstar is the force of darkness."

I'm the primordial force of light? What does that mean? Michael thought, unable to make sense of the revelation.

"This man here is one of the most powerful beings to ever grace the concept of existence. Rather, he used to be," she said with a devious grin to accompany the dark look on her face.

"What's with that grin?" Isabella asked in annoyance.

"Well, there's a bit of an issue in the prophecies," she started. "They say when Michael went onto his slumber; he lost all his powers and memories, so waking is a completely fresh start."

"Wait, so is that how Michael lost his memories?" Isabella asked.

She and Julianna looked over at him. He stared blankly as if his mind had numbed, unable to register her words.

This is not only who I was, but how I forgot.

Alexa let out a sinister chuckle as she turned to Michael. "You may have released your angel form, but you're no march for demons of our level of power!" She released her wings, and Ursula followed suit.

"And we'll do anything in our power to protect the rings from all evil," she continued, beating her wings against the dusty air.

"Does that also include you?" said Isabella.

"I can assure you our intentions are purer than you think," Alexa replied.

"And yet you plan on kidnapping me and hurting my friend to get what you want," Michael said, angrily.

Alexa looked into his eyes and smiled. "You act so high and mighty. Demons are morally loose, by nature. Sure, we may break a few souls here and there, but as long as we don't destroy the entire world, we're just fine."

"Pathetic!" Michael shouted with emphasis. "Like the archangel and what you claim to be the primordial force of light, I'll decide what's fine and what's not."

"What an arrogant little angel. If a battle is what you're after, then a battle you'll get," said Alexa.

"It's about time," Michael said, pointing his scepter at Alexa.

"Oh, but you won't be battling me," she replied.

"And why not?" Michael said with a piercing glare into her eyes.

"I'm out of your league. Battling me is not a right. It's a privilege. If you want the chance to battle me, you'll need to defeat Ursula, first," she said, pointing over at Ursula.

Michael looked at Ursula, still recovering from when Alexa knocked her to the ground.

"That is ridiculous. She's clearly still hurt," he refuted.

Ursula chimed in, "It's fine. I can take it. I'm not afraid of you."

"That's not the point. You don't have to listen to her. Don't you have any will of your own? Or any self-respect?" Michael pleaded.

"Maybe I don't. So, what?" Ursula asked.

Michael, Isabella, and Julianna looked at her. Her unbridled loyalty to Alexa made their heads spin.

"Enough stalling. Are we going stand and twiddle our thumbs all day or are we going to dance?" Ursula demanded, pointing at Michael.

Michael realized there was no way he would talk her out of it. Her mindless devotion to Alexa was beyond repair. He could see this in her change of tone. He still maintained concern and determination that she could change.

"If a battle's what you want, a battle's what you'll get! Maybe then, we can figure out what's really going on between you and that pink-haired freak."

Michael and Ursula squared off, exchanging a lightning-sharp stare. The atmosphere of silent tension left Julianna and Isabella watching with unease, while Alexa looked at Ursula, forging a grin that told of many secrets about the blue-haired girl.

CHAPTER 3
FANGS OF A CRYING WOLF

Michael looked sharply into Ursula's eyes. Her presence was no longer as childish and innocent as before. A sincere resolve replaced the childish and innocent presence Ursula once held. The thunderous gaze she now had left his heart racing with fear.

"You don't have to do this, Ursula. I really think you should rest," Michael said.

"I don't need you treating me like a child. I fell, is all," Ursula snapped.

"You didn't fall. She pushed you to the ground. And I'm not treating you like a child. I'm just saying"—

"I know what you're saying. I shouldn't do what Alexa says just to appease her. I should think of myself, instead. Well, you know what? I'm happy to do exactly that. And today, I'll take you as our captive and rob your orange-haired pal of her titan ring," Ursula snapped.

"Hey, I have a name. It's Isabella," she said, annoyed.

"And my name's Julianna. Thanks for asking..." she said with sarcasm.

"Is this really the time?" asked Michael, looking over at them.

"Sorry," they said, in unison.

"The rules of this battle are simple," Alexa interjected. "This will be one on one. No one outside is to interfere."

"And does that include you?" Julianna asked with a stern glare in Alexa's direction.

Alexa grinned. "Well, of course."

"That works for me," Julianna said.

"Finish this fast," Isabella chanted.

Michael turned his attention back at Ursula. "I'll let you make the first move, Ursula."

"Don't patronize me. Just because I'm a woman doesn't mean I need any favors from the likes of you!" she said, her face reddening in anger.

Just what is her deal? Michael thought. The longer he stared into her flaring expression, the more confused he grew. *I took her as the sort who had her head high in the clouds, but now it seems something has ignited a fire inside her. Did Alexa actually slap some sense into her or are these her true colors? Either way, despite our common desire to have Lucifer gone, there's little chance of us joining forces.*

Michael took a deep breath. "Fine, I'll go first. And if you don't want any favors, then I won't hold back."

"What a brute. Fine, go first"—Before Ursula could finish her sentence, Michael swung at her with his scepter, knocking her right over in the blink of an eye.

"I'm so sorry. I didn't think you'd fall that easily," Michael said in a panicked tone.

Isabella sighed from the sidelines. "What did that jackass think would happen after she fell to a single slap?"

"It seems he hasn't gotten his archangel powers under control yet. I blame his negligence towards his training," Julianna added.

Ursula limped up to her feet and dusted herself off. She stared, hypnotized by his worried glare. A tear rolled down her face as she stood up.

"Well, you didn't have to hit me with that thing. And so hard. I mean, who hits someone with a scepter? That's like hitting me across the head with a sword or an ax," said Ursula. She winced as she rubbed her bruised arm.

"I assumed you'd block it. I really am sorry," he replied.

"Dickhead!" Ursula shouted in defiance.

Michael offered a rain of apologies, offering to aid her injury with a healing potion. Ursula replied with a slew of expletives as Alexa snickered in amusement.

Meanwhile, Julianna and Isabella stared dimly.

"Well, this battle's going nowhere fast. One mediocre assault and his opponent's already crying," said Isabella.

"My thoughts, exactly," said Julianna.

"What is it?" asked Isabella. She could tell something was bothering Julianna.

"That girl. Something's not right in her head," she said.

"Yeah, I don't know if she just doesn't have a clue or if she actually just spent her entire life living with the dogs," Isabella said, staring intensely at Ursula.

"That's not what I meant. Didn't you notice a serious shift in her personality once Alexa pushed her into this battle?" said Julianna, with an instigative tone.

"I did," Isabella replied with a colder gaze. "Something tells me there's far more to this woman than meets the eye."

"But, the real danger is that Alexa woman. It's clear she has Ursula wrapped around her finger. Michael had better be careful not to find himself in the same position. Especially when our only titan ring is on the line," said Julianna.

"Agreed," Isabella said with an affirmative nod.

Meanwhile, Alexa eavesdropped on their conversation

while watching Michael and Ursula fail to bury their hostilities.

"You imbeciles can try to figure me out all you want. You're wasting your time. The queen of the sixth dimension is beyond both your comprehension and your power. When this is all over, I'll take your titan ring and this sad excuse for the archangel all to myself," said Alexa to herself, grinning, as she looked over at Ursula.

"If you're done trying to heal with your weird angel magic, you can back up," Ursula dusted herself off and took a deep breath.

"Weird?" Michael said in a baffled tone.

"What are you waiting for?" Alexa shouted. "Attack that moron now!"

Ursula took a deep breath and nodded. She stared up at Michael with a callous gaze. "Right."

Taking Michael by surprise, she opened her assault with a bare fist. She lunged forward and struck him across the chest, nearly knocking him over.

Michael grunted in pain. He pressed against the sharp pain in his chest.

"A punch? That certainly wasn't what I expected," he said with a pant.

"Unlike some people, I don't need swords or axes to fight." Ursula raised both her fist towards him as she dug back her heel. "I may not look like much, but I'm one hell of a fighter. And I've never needed weapons to get where I am."

Michael's eyes widened. The determination she wore emanated deeper. He could almost feel it coursing through her veins.

"I never meant to undermine your capabilities. I'm sorry. If your fists are your weapon of choice, that's alright with me. I'm sure you'll prove to be a challenge for me, regardless." Michael replied with a friendly smile.

Ursula gazed at him with bewilderment. She smiled and nodded. "Good. Then get ready because I've got a real beating prepared with your name on it."

"Bring it!" Michael thrust forward with his scepter firmly in his grasp. Ursula did the same with her fists. Like an impulse, Ursula mirrored with her hands balled. Primed and ready to fight.

The two clashed amidst the peaceful cornfield. Ursula drove a barrage of punches at Michael, but he deflected with his scepter.

"Not bad." Michael smiled.

He returned the attack with the same bravado as before, ready to further his advantage in their skirmish.

"Well, I can do better. Way better."

Ursula parried before countering with a thudding fist to his belly. A grin formed across her face as he leaned over, aching.

Julianna and Isabella observed, growing even more baffled.

"Using your fists against a scepter is pretty unorthodox, don't you think?" Isabella asked.

"In the assassin trade, it's typical to use light weaponry against something heavier. For example, a dagger against a claymore. But using bare fists is extreme unless you build a career in pummeling people in alleyways," Julianna said.

"That could explain the sort of fighter she is and why Alexa seems to keep her around, despite disliking her," said Isabella.

"A secret weapon, perhaps?" Julianna said. She looked over at the rage building in Ursula's eyes before meeting the malice carried in Alexa's. "I fear greater obstacles than a woman fearless enough to face the archangels with her fists await us."

"You're right." Isabella's heart skipped a beat as she turned her attention towards Ursula's eyes. The aura within was enough to consume one whole. "Let's not forget they have three titan rings between them."

"And I'm certain Ursula carries one of them," Julianna said.

Julianna and Isabella relayed their suspicion while the heat of the battle between Michael and Ursula raged on. Michael limited his attack and defense to the swing of his scepter, wielding it like a spear. He avoided the use of magic at all costs. Ursula continued to fight barehanded, smirking under her breath. "You may think you can keep up with that golden rod of yours, but I've fought beasts larger than you with my bare hands countless times. You're no match for me."

She unleashed a thick and inky shadowlike substance from the crevices between her fingers. It hung over her fists like black clouds. She thumped Michael across the face with such force that he fell over.

"Michael!" Julianna and Isabella shouted.

Alexa snickered in amusement. "There's your fighting spirit. Don't let me down if you know what's good for you," she told Ursula.

Michael slowly rose with his face aching across the cheek. "I'll be fine. Hell knows I've taken worse hits."

He looked over at Ursula's fists and saw the shadows forming around them. He could sense the aura burning through her fingers like untamable magma, growing more furious the longer they waited.

"Though I can't say I've been hit quite like that," Michael said.

"I'm ready to raise the stakes if you are, Michael." Ursula grinned.

Michael smirked. Strings of electricity coursed from his scepter, igniting the dusty air.

"If a battle of magic is what you're looking for, that's fine with me. I could use the training."

"You'll get that and so much more with me. Trust me." Ursula warned.

She hurled herself back into the battlefield with a blackened storm around her fists. Grinning, Michael struck with his scepter. He clashed his lightning against her shadows, sending the battlefield in a fist of molten black and white.

Alexa, Julianna, and Isabella shielded their eyes from the impact. As the smoke settled, they peaked over their arms to see the battle continue. The state of the battle brought expressions of dread onto some and elation onto another as Ursula appeared to gain the advantage.

Michael and Ursula rushed through the battlefield, sending it in a frenzy of magic energy. Ursula punched and kicked her way through the voltage, breaking forth a path with her shadow magic as Michael unfurled convulsing streams with one ferocious grunt and a swing of his scepter after another.

"I must admit ... you're a tough one," Michael said with a heavy pant as he continued to thrust his scepter in her direction.

"Don't patronize me. Or do you just enjoy complimenting your opponents?" Ursula asked, veraciously countering back with her darkened fists.

"Perhaps." Michael thought back to one of his past battles —his first as the archangel—against the three elementals. "I've defeated much larger adversaries, as well. Strong as you are, it'll take a lot more than fists and shadow magic to defeat me." Michael said, matter-of-factly, as his attacks inched towards her face.

"You don't say," she replied.

She grabbed his scepter by its head, stopping it in its track. "Formidable as your previous skirmishes may have been, none could compare to the denizen I have in store for you, Michael."

"Do it! End this now!" Alexa shouted with a grin.

"As you wish," Ursula said.

Michael responded, "Wait, what are you talking about?"

"I feared this would happen," Julianna said.

"Michael, watch out!" Isabella exclaimed. "She's going to summon one of her titans."

Michael gasped. His chest tightened as the skies went black and the wind suddenly grew stronger. He watched with terror dawning over the once glowing horizon as a purple ring appeared on her finger.

"I should have known you'd resort to using a titan ring. A shame you're willing to take this battle so far," Michael said.

"There's no distance I won't travel for Alexa," she refuted.

"But, why? What are you getting out of your relationship with her?" Michael pressed. He looked over at Alexa, hoping to get an explanation. Instead, she responded with a disinterested and far-off gaze.

"The nature of our bond doesn't concern you. If I were you, I'd be more worried about the titan," Ursula shouted.

"A titan," Michael muttered. He tried to envision such a towering beast—one capable of inciting fear and domination among all those that sought them. He shuddered at the notion of three being in her possession.

"And once I summon him, it'll all be over for you," Ursula warned him with a confidently dark smile.

"Don't do this," Michael pleaded.

"It's too late," Ursula announced. The skies erupted as a vortex manifested among the swirling clouds above. "You had your chance to give up your ring when you did. Now, you must suffer for your disobedience."

"You haven't any idea what you're doing. A power like this could"—

"It matters not what happens to your world," Alexa interjected before Julianna could finish. "This is the devastation our rings carry and the resolution we possess in collecting the others. If you won't back down, this is your fate."

The phenomenon in the sky spread far and wide, for all to see. Villages of both kingdoms took notice, falling into a wave of panic. The people fled into their homes, screaming and closing their doors with the sounds of roars in the clouds.

This is a resolution to serve you, Ursula thought. *Terrified as I am, I'll do this to make you happy with me.*

Isabella and Julianna looked over at Ursula, noticing her fist trembling as she raised it towards the clouds.

"She's afraid?" They both thought.

Michael's eyes widened from fear. His lips quivered as the darkness dragged him to the brink of terror. Even the surrounding sounds seemed to be swallowed by the terror of something monolithic approaching. He felt his mind slipping away, then the sounds of shouts snapped him back.

"Don't worry, Michael. If I can take one down, so can you," Isabella shouted.

"Yes, we believe in you. Now, take this blue-haired psychopath out, already," Julianna added.

Michael looked at their smiling faces, disoriented for a moment before taking a deep breath and smiling back. "Thank you."

He then looked back over at Ursula, noticing the fear in her. Despite his readiness to speak out again, he knew she would ignore him. He bit back his anguish and looked the other way.

"What's that face for?" Ursula asked. "Are you intimidated by my power?"

Michael looked back, gritting his teeth. "Summon your titan if that's what you want. As long as there's someone who believes in me, I won't back down."

Ursula smiled. The winds grew stronger and the ground

below them broke with the emergence of glowing black fissures.

"A most foolish mistake."

Ursula smiled as she looked down at the ground. The wind blew through her hair. With a deep breath, she raised her ring-bearing fist high, preparing to chant in her titan's arrival.

"Oh, mighty beast of Transylvanian delight. Rise from your shallow grave and lead the pack to victory. Never will those from such inferior realms question your might again. Come forth! Lycanthrope, titan of the second dimension!"

With the end of her chant, came a painful pause and silence filled the air. The winds halted, and the ground appeared to calm in place. Until suddenly, a furry hand clad in bloody claws emerged from below, in a chasm of infinite darkness. Michael watched, in horror, as a beast grander than any he'd ever seen pulled itself onto the surface.

"Is that"—Michael said, nearly falling over at the sight.

"Yes! The last titan you'll ever see!" Ursula stood before the titan: a giant werewolf with sharp fangs and jagged spikes on its back. It stood hundreds of feet, reaching for the clouds.

"Oh, no. It's the biggest creature I've ever seen!" said Michael.

"That's right. Now, go my beast. Attack him with your Transylvanian howling!" Ursula commanded. The beast howled at the emerging full moon as what remained of the day slipped into the night. The titan's unyielding stomp created shockwaves across the battlefield that nearly broke the land below them once again.

Blocking his ears, Michael could no longer concentrate on his fighting. "What a roar on that beast!"

The damaging sounds of Lycanthrope battered Julianna and Isabella too as they pushed against their ears in defense.

Alexa looked up with glistening eyes. A grin formed across her face.

Ursula called off the beast's howl and smiled. Calming down, Michael took his hands down from his ears and looked back at her. He breathed heavily as his eyes shook from the intensity of the werewolf's unbridled rage.

"Why did you stop?"

Ursula looked at him with a callous glare. "That's the power of this titan. It came from an age when powerful undead creatures known as vampires ruled the world. Then one day, they waged war with another powerful undead race known as the werewolves. Both seeking absolute control of the dimension, they fought until there was only one victor. That victor was the vampires."

"Why are you telling me this?" Michael asked

"Because this titan is a reminder of its ancestors' defeat by the hands of their enemy, forced to live the rest of its days as nothing more than a servant to one's bidding. In this case, mine."

"That may all be well and true, but I'll still find a way to defeat it!" Michael confidently said as he gazed up at the snarling beast.

"Fat chance. This creature comes from a whole other world. One I doubt you can remember," said Ursula.

Michael smiled. "I don't need to. You said it, yourself. The vampires could defeat the werewolves," he said.

"What's your point?" Ursula asked, confused and annoyed.

"My point is; if they can be destroyed once, then they can be destroyed again!" said Michael.

Ursula looked at him and snickered. "How arrogant. Do you realize how much stronger a titan is, compared to a simple pack of werewolves? You'll die for those words, just like the other disgusting hounds. Lycanthrope, attack with your spine crushing claw!"

The largest hand Michael had ever seen—a paw large enough to take out an entire building—came straight for him and met him.

Michael pointed his scepter towards the beast's hand, harvesting electricity from the stormy skies like a lightning rod.

The electricity reached the tip of his scepter, only fading into the darkness upon arrival. "What's happening?"

"I guess the howl from my beast was so loud, your scepter didn't hear you call out to it!" said Ursula, smiling. "Maybe try something else. That is if you can. And fast."

Michael watched the gaping paw break through the atmosphere, reaching toward him with a blackened pulse surrounding it. Trembling with fear, he gritted his teeth and attempted to evade its traps with flight, only to find that his wings were just as unresponsive.

"My wings, they won't work!"

He evaded the assault just in time. His inability to fly didn't make an ounce of sense to him.

"I suppose you're not the archangel of legend you once were. Once you're in range of its howling attack, it renders your flight capabilities worthless and will be for the rest of our battle. Oh, well," said Ursula.

Michael's widened gaze wasn't going anywhere as the titan came straight for him.

"We have to do something," Isabella screamed.

"You recall the rules Alexa made. No one is to interfere," Julianna replied.

"But"—

"If we were to step in, that would give Alexa the excuse to do the same. And with two more titans in their possession we can't afford to take that risk," Julianna explained.

The reality set in for Isabella as she stared at the undying smirk across Alexa's face.

"In that case, Michael will have to brace the attack," Isabella said.

Julianna nodded as they both watched the descent of the titan's hand with anxiety swelling.

"Great work, Ursula. You've made me proud today." A proudly smiling Alexa said.

The titan's hand crashed like an earthquake. Michael screamed in pain when he took the full force of the devastation. Julianna and Isabella shrieked with terror. The fear locked them in place.

The fist rose from the ground, leaving its ruins behind. Michael laid there, unconscious and swept away by his self-doubt, phasing out the cries from his friends, as they ran to his aid.

My powers. They failed me.

The attack transported Michael to the darkest part of his mind, once again. He gazed around, questioning what had just occurred.

Was I not good enough? Was it my destiny to lose? And who is that Ursula woman to Alexa? What does she want out of her?

※

SUDDENLY, HIS EYES BURST OPEN TO THE SIGHT OF ISABELLA and Julianna tending to him.

"Impossible! No one's ever survived an attack from that titan," said Ursula.

"You fool. He's not just anyone. He's the archangel!" said Alexa.

"You're right. My mistake." Ursula tightened her fists. "My titan will just have to attack harder."

"I'm so glad you're alright." Isabella helped him to his feet, gripping him in her arms. "I was so worried about you!"

"Likewise, my sweet Michael," Julianna said, doing the same.

"I appreciate your concern. Thank you." With their help, Michael returned to his feet and fixed a stern gaze at Ursula.

"I don't know what's going on between you two, but it ends today. Titan or not, you're both finished!" Michael declared.

Ursula and Alexa responded with a stunned look. "Finished? Surely, you jest!" Alexa shouted. "You can't fly and your scepter doesn't even work anymore. The only one here who's finished is you!"

"You're wrong. As soon as I break this little partnership of yours, it's all over," said Michael.

"I beg your pardon?" Alexa replied.

Michael set his sights back at Ursula. "Ursula, why is it you stand by such a cruel woman. I want to know."

"My decisions are none of your concern," Ursula insisted.

"I'm aware of that. And I know I can't force you to do anything you don't want to do, but just hear me out. I grew up in a house where the highlight of my day was hiding from my masters, hoping to avoid my regular beatings, even if it meant two beatings the next day," said Michael.

Ursula went into silent thought. "What's your point, Michael?" she demanded. She tried but failed to hold back tears from trickling down her face.

"I'm saying you don't have to live that abusive lifestyle. I escaped it and so can you. Now, the master I once hated is one of my closest friends." Michael looked at Isabella and smiled. Taken by surprise, Isabella looked back and blushed.

"What are you trying to tell me?" Ursula said, now trembling in her voice. "That Alexa is abusive? That I didn't deserve to be hit?"

Michael paused in disbelief. He remembered the bruises

Hecate wore across her arm, wondering if Lucifer manipulated her to feel the same way.

"I'm telling you it's not too late to stand up to your inner demons, Ursula. More importantly, I want you to take a stand against Alexa and show her you're your own person who can make your own decisions in life," said Michael.

"My own person?" Ursula wondered.

"Yes, if there's anything I've learned from my past battles, it's that the life you live is your own. No one can take that from you," said Michael.

He recalled his encounter with Hecate and contemplated the way she left their world. The parallels were as similar to him as they were frightening.

"My own life." Ursula pondered with reluctance. The malice she held within melted.

Taking notice of her calming demeanor, Alexa gritted her teeth.

"Don't listen to him. He's full of shit. Do you want that imbecile as your master or would you rather stay with me? Just think of the life I've given you. He'll never be able to do the same!"

"The only life you've given her is one of abuse and broken self-confidence," said Michael.

Alexa responded, "You know nothing!"

"She clearly never wanted to fight me and is only doing this because you ordered her to," he said with a ferocious look. He then focused his attention back on Ursula, doing his best to calm himself.

"You don't have to be submissive to anyone. Don't serve her and definitely don't serve me. Just serve yourself from now on," he said with a welcoming smile.

"Serve myself?" asked Ursula.

"Yes. Learn to respect yourself, Ursula. Otherwise, you'll

get stepped on by bullies like Alexa your entire life," he said, looking over at a sneering Alexa.

"Respect myself?" Ursula said as if none of this ever occurred to her.

"Yes You're a kind person. I can sense that. Dig deep and you can find the will to embrace that kindness and leave that darkness behind," he said with an assuring smile.

Alexa watched with a thundering scowl. With her jaws clenched, her breaths grew fierce. Julianna and Isabella held back tears, basking in the warmth of Michael's interaction with Ursula.

"Michael truly is a compassionate spirit. Even going as far as aiding his adversary," said Julianna.

"And for good reason," Isabella added, "We're after the same thing. When push comes to shove, we'd be better off colluding."

Ursula looked around her. The gazes piercing through her from every direction trapped her. She took a deep breath to calm her frantic breathing.

"I can't."

"Yes, you can. You just have to try"—

"I can't!" said Ursula, cutting Michael off, as a fit of panic came over her.

The ground beneath them crumbled away as the debris levitated. Ursula screamed in pain.

"Ursula, listen to me!" Michael pleaded.

"What's happening to her?" Julianna asked with a frightened stare.

"This anger. I vaguely remember feeling this way during my battle with Hecate, but it was all so hazy." Isabella desperately tried to recall it.

"You've done it now. I hope you're happy!" said Alexa.

Ursula's aura grew as she shattered the surrounding debris.

She looked at Michael with blaring crimson eyes as the surrounding sclera blackened.

"You won't brainwash me, Michael. I'm tired of listening to what others tell me. Whether it's you or Alexa, I'm done."

"But, that's what I've been saying all along. Just be yourself. Not what someone wants you to be," said Michael.

Those eyes. Is she also an etherial demon? Isabella thought.

"I was told for so many years that the *me* I was born as was not worth being," Ursula said, shedding a tear.

"That's terrible. No one should ever be denied who they are," said Michael.

"But Alexa she gave me a chance," Ursula argued.

"No, you gave her a chance and she failed you," Michael refuted. "Ursula, I saw the real you before our battle. An unusual, yet very innocent and endearing woman who just wants to smile. That is the real you. Not this insecure and enraged mess."

"How could you know that was the real me?" Ursula shouted. "You really think you know me?"

"I have a feeling about these things. I can't say for sure, but I sense you're a great girl with many wonderful qualities. I'm sure anyone would be happy to call you their friend," said Michael.

"Me? A friend?" Ursula pondered, crying tears of joy.

"Yes, and if you'd like, I could be your friend." Michael walked over to her and reached out his hand.

Ursula ambled up to him, with each step echoing in her hesitant heart until it opened. She looked up into his eyes and broke down even more. She hugged him with a zealous grip.

"You have no idea how long I've waited for something like this. Something to mend my long-broken heart after so many years of torment."

"Ursula, what are you doing?" Alexa trembled with

outrage from the show of affection. "Think of what I've given you."

"You should think of what you've taken away from her," Michael refuted.

Cradling Ursula's head in his chest, he looked down into her still blackened eyes and smiled. Ursula put her hand across his face and smiled.

"My friend." She smiled then kissed him on the lips, evoking gasps and dropped jaws.

"Hey, get your whorish face off him!" Isabella shouted.

"That's my husband!" Julianna demanded.

The two of them ran towards her and Michael, ready to peel her off his body with haste and aggravation.

Michael's eyes widened from the touch of her lips. *This isn't what friends do*. He was ready to push her away but held back when he saw her eyes return to normal. Her assertion surprised him, but he was content with the elated look in her eyes. He took a deep breath and allowed her all the time she needed in his embrace.

In reaction, the titan descended back into the earth. Ursula dragged her lips away from his and stared at him with embarrassment.

"I'm sorry. Was that too forward?"

"Maybe a little," he replied with a nervous laugh.

"A little?" Isabella pulled her away by the back of the collar and stared at her with dagger-eyes. "I don't know what sort of shit hole you came from, but in this dimension, you don't go around kissing your friends."

"I'm sorry. Please don't hurt me." Ursula whimpered. "I don't want to fight anymore."

"After kissing my husband and attacking him with a titan, I'd say you have no other option," Isabella stated.

"Yes, believe it or not, but those things bother most women,' Julianna added.

Her fingers inched towards her infinity bag, ready to pull out any blade eager enough to quench her contempt.

"Easy, you two. She said she's sorry," said Michael.

"Says the man clearly flirting with her," Isabella replied.

"I admire your trusting heart, but you're too kind for your own good," Julianna stated.

"You might be right." Michael nodded. "Still. It helped Ursula see the error of her ways. And for me, that was worth it."

Julianna responded, "You have a point. Though, I still don't care for having another potential rival for your heart in my life."

"She could be useful, though. Another demon in our corner, along with a titan ring," said Isabella.

"And chances are she knows something about the Legion of Morningstar since she's been traveling with Alexa," Michael added.

"Yeah, I do," Ursula said. "Please let me join you guys."

"Will you promise to keep your lips to yourself?" Isabella asked.

"No guarantees," Ursula looked over at Michael with blushing cheeks.

"Well, you an audacious one," Julianna replied.

"I can make up for it by cooking all your meals," Ursula suggested.

Isabella smiled. "That doesn't sound like a bad idea."

"So, I can join you?" Ursula's eyes widened with childlike joy.

"I suppose another ally could be useful. What do you say?" Julianna asked. "Would you care to leave that stuck up woman behind?"

"You'll need to learn some basic manners too," said Isabella.

"Yes." Ursula smiled. "I'd love that."

"Then, it looks like we have a new friend and a helping hand in taking the demon king," said Michael.

Michael and his friends shared welcoming smiles with Ursula. Their moment of bliss nearly alienated Alexa's presence.

Alexa watched with a thundering look on her face.

How dare she betray me?

The anguish built into a raging tempest as darkness consumed her surroundings. She was going to show them why crossing her was a lethal mistake.

"I won't let you get away with this. When I'm finished, I'll not only have your ring but your heads too."

CHAPTER 4
BLIND LEADING THE BLIND

Smiles and laughter filled the atmosphere among Michael and his friends. Ursula's eyes glowed with a joy she hadn't felt in ages.

"Thank you again, Michael. Even though I was so cruel, you were still so kind to me."

"It was my pleasure. So long as you don't mind helping us out," Michael said.

"Of course." Ursula nodded.

"With you on our side, that makes two titans. The same as the demon king, himself." Julianna smiled.

"Perhaps now, we'll be evenly matched for when we meet." Michael thought back to Lucifer's statement and the ace he pulled. Certain she and her titan could help level the battlefield when the time came.

Their moment of celebration came to an abrupt end when Alexa marched over to Ursula. They all laid their unnerving eyes on her. She snatched Ursula from her grip on Michael and grabbed her by the front of her shirt.

"How dare you betray me like that? After everything I've done for you!"

"Hey, leave her alone," Michael shouted. "She's had more than enough of you."

"Ridiculous. This feeble woman has no will of her own. She simply does what her master says. And the only master she answers to is me!" Alexa hurled Ursula onto the dirt on the ground.

Michael watched Ursula whimper before meeting Alexa's contempt-filled eyes with unbridled outrage.

"How dare you? What the hell did that poor girl ever do to you?"

The anger inside Michael pushed him close to punching Alexa across the face, had it not been for Isabella and Julianna restraining him.

"Leave it alone, Michael. She isn't worth our time," said Isabella.

"She's right. Ursula may be manageable, but Alexa's insane. You don't want to get mixed up with her any longer," said Julianna.

"I don't care about any of that. Ursula's my friend. Let me go!" Michael refuted, attempting to break the hold they had on him.

"You, a friend of Ursula's? What a laugh!" Alexa scoffed at the very notion before kicking Ursula in the stomach. "People like her don't deserve friends, they only deserve pain!"

"Is that really what you think?" A blinding light emitted around Michael like a growing aura. It shone with such force; everyone nearly fell over.

Alexa shielded her eyes as the battlefield plunged into his relentless rays of light.

The light dimmed to reveal Michael in his archangel form. He stood with resentment burning fiercely in his eyes.

"That's enough, Alexa. Your fight is with me, now."

Alexa looked at him and grinned. "Well, I made a promise. And I always keep my word."

"Good. And if I win, you are to never lay a hand on Ursula again," Michael demanded.

Alexa snickered. "Well, when I win, I will make you my slave, as well. Fuck my previous talks of using you to bait out the Legion of Morningstar's leader. I want you to suffer at my own hands!"

"Take her, Michael!" Isabella exclaimed.

"Show this dimension jumping bitch you mean business," Julianna added.

"You don't have to tell me twice. If you could, though, I'd like you to take Ursula somewhere safe. Things are about to get ugly here." he said.

Julianna and Isabella smiled proudly as they did as he said, carrying her off to the sideline. Michael and Alexa now looked across from each other, matching each other's menacing glares, and foreboding auras sweeping the battlefield.

"So, how should we decide who makes the first move?"

"It matters not," Alexa replied, "I will win, either way. Don't forget I have our two remaining titans."

Michael gritted his teeth. "I haven't."

"Good." Alexa smiled. "If you'd like, however, you can make the first move. After all, a dirty angel with amnesia could use the head start."

"You'll live to regret those words!" Michael burst forward, charging towards her with his scepter drawn. The ground sparked with heavy voltage.

Alexa grinned, just before grabbing the tip of the scepter, stopping him in place. "Do you honestly expect to defeat me with this little toy? This thing may work against familiars and other weak specimens, but I'm of a whole other breed." Alexa snatched the scepter out of his hand and hurled it into the dirt.

Michael saw his reflection in his scepter sticking out of

the ground beside him. He then diverted his attention back to Alexa but was too late. She hit him with a weapon of her own.

Her assault knocked the wind clean out of him. He gasped for breath while his ears rang with each painstaking moment he took to rise. Michael immediately noticed the colossal bronze mallet in her hold as the sunshine reflected off it.

"Impressed? This hammer of mine is an unholy relic," Alexa said.

"You mean you own two titans and an unholy relic?"

Michael's eyes widened. He doubted if he had the might it would take to turn this fight around, but he would not let up. He could neither allow her to see the doubt nor give her the advantage. Not now, not ever.

"That may be true for now, but when this is over, I'll have four titans. Goodbye!" Alexa shouted, slamming the head of her weapon onto an already struggling Michael, sending him back to the ground.

"Michael, no!" Ursula pleaded.

She and Michael's friends looked away. They couldn't bear the sight of his body being crushed by the weight of Alexa's hammer.

"It's over, Michael. I win," Alexa declared with a triumphant grin.

Suddenly, the hammer jerked in her hands. It rose from the ground. Ursula and Michael's friends smiled in shock and relief as Michael pushed his way out from under the hammer.

"You still dare to defy me?" asked Alexa.

"Not everyone lives to serve you. That's called free will and everyone has the right to it, whether you like it or not." With one last thrust, Michael hurled Alexa's hammer out of her hands and high into the sky.

"My unholy relic!" It landed over a dozen feet away—far too much a distance for her reach before he could strike.

"You insolent angel swine." Alexa struck a punch at Michael. Before it could land, he caught it. Alexa looked in his eyes, stunned and nervous, as her second attack came to a halt.

"The tides are changing, Alexa. I suggest you forfeit now and leave before I really hurt you," said Michael.

This man is so much more intense than I thought he'd be. Could he have already regained his powers? It feels like he's holding back. Alexa thought, shaking as she looked into his cold blue eyes.

Meanwhile, everyone else stood on the sidelines, watching intensely as the battle unfolded. Isabella had just put the finishing touches of her healing magic on Ursula. She now stood upright and watched with a confident smile.

"Thanks, Isabella," Ursula said.

"Anytime," she replied.

Julianna kept her attention on the battle before them. "Ursula, give me your honest opinion. What do you think Michael's chances are of winning?"

Isabella kept her eyes on Ursula, hoping for good news.

"Not good, I'm afraid. Alexa's completely undefeated. Not to mention, she hates angels, so we can expect her to go at him even more aggressively than she normally would."

"Figures as much since she's a demon." Julianna scowled.

"Our aligning with him should be enough to show we can trust him. Why is she going so far for control?" Isabella asked.

"She's not one to take 'no' for an answer. I don't think she's ever not gotten what she wanted," Ursula replied.

Julianna gulped. "In that case, I hope Michael has some sort of surprise to tip the outcome in his favor."

"Well, Michael's the archangel. Demons and angels may

be enemies in most stories and tales, but I, for one, believe in him," said Julianna.

"That's right. As long as we're here to support him, he can't lose!" Isabella added.

Their confidence painted a stunned look on Ursula's face. She smiled. "He must mean a lot to you guys."

"He does," Isabella began. "That man is my world. We grew up together in the same house. I just wish I hadn't treated him how I did all those years, though. We lost so much time that we could have spent growing our love together. To make up for this, I have dedicated my life to prove to him that I am worthy of his love."

Ursula stared at her in silence before turning towards Alexa. "So, you hurt him, but you still love him?"

She watched as she continued to combat Michael ruthlessly. Wondering if her movement carried any of the same compassion.

"I do. With all my heart." Isabella said, smiling.

A smile formed across Ursula's face, mesmerized by Isabella's words and the motions of the battlefield.

"Michael holds great significance to me, as well," Julianna said. "I've never met a man so well-mannered to women before. As you've seen for yourself, when he cares about you, he'll spare no time showing it. Good men are tough to come by. A great man like him, well, you just don't let someone like that go."

Ursula's eyes widened. She looked over at Michael with a firm nod and a smile, determined to make him see her the same way the others see him.

Meanwhile, the battle between Michael and Alexa raged on. They exchanged bloody, bone-crunching blows, and devastating displays of supernatural power.

"Just how much longer do you plan on keeping up this

charade?" Alexa said as she sent dark bursts of magic energy his way.

He deflected the energy with his arm and returned a confident look at her. "As long as it takes to prove to you that your way will never succeed."

He manifested his sword from his hand. The iron gleam took Alexa by surprise. The voltage seeped from the blade's edge and fired towards her like a lightning strike piercing the darkness.

Alexa swiftly dodged it and frowned.

"I'll admit, I didn't expect that sword. Perhaps you haven't completely lost your touch." Alexa began. "Even so, who do you think you are telling me what the right way is? I'm the richest and most powerful woman to ever grace the sixth dimension. My power and influence are absolute. There is only one way: my way."

Michael sneered at her words, recalling his conversation with Lucifer in their dream. His heart thundered just as it did then.

"You talk about wealth and power, but where has that gotten you?"

"Excuse me?" Alexa demanded.

"I'd imagine someone with your influence sending out her servants to collect the titan ring in your stead," Michael stated.

"You think I'd ever trust someone with such a critical task? And let the ring fall in the hands of inferior soldiers?" Alexa refuted.

"As a matter of fact, I don't," Michael replied. "Because I think the only person you trust is Ursula. And since she's left you behind, that means you're"—

"Shut the fuck up!" Alexa's eyes flared with malice. Her blackened aura spread around like ink shattering the air.

The hair on Michael's neck stood upright. "It means you're all alone. Just as I was."

"Like hell I am," Alexa shouted. "I have everything I need."

"To her point, she does still possess two titans," Isabella began.

"And if Michael continues to provoke her, he'll find himself face to face against one or both very soon."

I can't let her become absorbed in her tyranny, Michael thought, *or she'll end up like Lucifer.*

"I think it's time I teach the archangel a lesson for speaking out against the queen." Alexa unfurled sharp talons from each of her fingertips. They sliced through the air, dripping down dark magical energy across the grass.

And I can't let her do this alone. Because then, she'll end up like me. Michael thought as the memories of solitude and vilification still tore at him.

Alexa unfurled her wings, beating them against her shadows. She spread out her sharp talons and rushed towards Michael, prepared to let her fury erupt.

"You're wrong!" Michael blocked the wall of shadows she formed by slicing through with his blade. The intensity sent her flying and landing on her back.

"You disgusting brute! What sort of attack breaks through my shadows like that?" Alexa grunted as she slowly picked herself.

"I'd appreciate it if you'd stop insulting me," Michael replied. "Your poor attitude may get you wealth and power, but there is more to life than that. Take it from someone who's never had either of those things."

Alexa coughed and panted when she stood back up. She rounded a look at the mutiny and resentment in everyone's eyes. Her face reddened. "I've had enough of you. All of you.

If I hear one more word from you or the others about friendship and believing yourself, I'm going to fucking lose it!"

"Then, by all means, lose it," Michael replied with a sneer.

Alexa's eyes narrowed as he touched the last of her nerves. "I'll mark your grave with those words." Familiar otherworldly energy shrouded the battlefield—the same one the titan of the second dimension carried.

Michael's heart raced as darkness surrounded him. He looked around at the terrified gazes to his left and over at her.

"Everyone's afraid now." He began. "And that's your doing. Do you still wish to continue?"

"You're mistaken, Michael. I'm ending this. Right here and now," she said as a purple ring appeared around her finger.

"I see." Michael tightened his grip on his sword. "I suppose we both are."

Suddenly, the clouds in the sky opened, revealing the same pitch-black whirlpool of thunderous darkness that came with the second dimension titan. Lightning filled the air above, as Michael watched, horrified by the call of the beast from the sky.

"Mighty bird that hunts the dead. May you grace our killing grounds and rob my foe of all its life. Come forth! Tiamat, titan of the first dimension!"

With her chant's conclusion, the sky responded with claps of lightning. A blue humanoid vulture broke through the writhing clouds, descending from the blackened heavens. The beast's wings spanned across the skies, sending gusts roaring past with every flap. A terrified Julianna backed off as she watched. Isabella froze while her heart did all the running. Ursula swallowed heavy breaths to calm her jitters.

"Holy shit, that's an enormous bird!" Michael said, stunned, as it landed before them and trembled the ground in its wake.

"Yes my dimension titan is here, at last!" said Alexa.

The beast stood tall, with massive feathered wings, two arms, and two legs. It cawed to the heavens, shaking the weeping sky into a lightning-induced rage.

Michael gazed into its soulless eyes, mesmerized by its energy. "What an incredible beast!"

Alexa grinned. "Just wait and see what it can do!" The beast soared into the air, circling the battlefield.

"What's it doing?" Michael asked.

He found himself quickly mesmerized by its sweeping motions—like the hands of a clock moving around the face without ever missing a second.

"In prehistoric times, the world was covered in nothing, but ferocious beasts," Alexa began. "To survive, you had to be strong. You had to be vigilant and do whatever was necessary to survive. There was no use for weak emotions, as those pitiful humans weren't around yet to plague our world with such things. No, if you wanted to survive, you had to be the best at everything you did. And as I speak, Tiamat is preparing to prove its top slot on the food chain by delivering a strike upon you."

"We'll just see about that." Michael raised his sword high, ready to combat the impact of the titan.

"While vultures usually only attack the dead, it can make an exception for a dead man walking."

"How very charming. And you wonder why I wanted to break Ursula away from you." Michael sneered.

"Revel in that petty victory." Alexa looked up at her titan with a smile. "You're the one who's on the chopping block. And by the looks of it, Tiamat's about to feed!"

The vulture soared high into the air. Everyone's hearts trembled in fear as they watched the beast look directly down at Michael with hollow black eyes, like the night, before flying down at a speed beyond sound.

"Oh, no!" he said, in disbelief of its pace and ferocity.

"Oh, yes! Now go, my servant. Feed on this weak excuse for an angel," Alexa called.

Before the titan could strike, Michael stopped it in its tracks, forcing all the light energy that he could onto it from his sword by jabbing the blade between its teeth.

"What do you think you're doing?" Alexa asked, flustered at the sight of her servant attempting to gnaw through the lightning coursing through Michael's blade. Its teeth could not break through the blockade.

"Stopping your titan's assault," said Michael.

"You now dare to challenge the might of a dimension titan with that weak magic of yours?" Alexa responded.

"Say what you want about my magic, but so long as my friends stand by me, I'll never give up. Not on me and not on them," said Michael.

Julianna and Isabella cheered in support of his resistance. Ursula soon joined them before turning away at Alexa's scornful glare.

"You cannot stop my dimension titan, Michael. Forfeit or I will use it to crush you!" Alexa shouted with as much vitriol as she could express.

"We'll just see about that." Michael ran his sword deep through the beast's gullet. The lightning pulsating from the blade filled its mouth.

Alexa watched with disbelief as the once-mighty titan faltered. Its movements slowed, and the lightning took hold.

My servant, too? Her eyes widened. She remembered many tireless nights reading all the spell books she could get a hold of, each regarding the history of the archangel. *Everything I've ever come to know about him is false. His power is just as it was all those years ago. He's a monster.*

"You can do it, Michael!" Julianna shouted.

"Send that giant vulture back to the first dimension where it came from," Isabella exclaimed.

Michael smiled, feeling the last of the bird's fight give in to the ruthless of lightning in his sword.

"Gladly."

With a tightening and one swing, he knocked the titan high into the sky. His friends watched as it slowly fell in a fit of electrocution before he cast it into the ground. Alexa's eyes widened from shock as a gaping crater formed with its defeat.

"Get up, you worthless titan. We still have work to do!" The titan roared in pain as it slowly got up in a limp state.

"You don't respect anyone or anything, do you?" said Michael.

"Stop pretending you fucking know me. Nobody asked for more of your preachy bullshit," said Alexa.

"Tell me, Alexa. How did you come across Ursula?" he asked.

"What do you mean?" Alexa asked in annoyance.

"You two come from very different dimensions, right? I don't fully understand how dimensions work yet, but that seems like some distance to go for someone you don't respect. Just how did you two come together?"

"You don't know when to shut that mouth of yours, do you?" Alexa gritted her teeth. "You really want to know? Fine."

She remembered the experience in her home dimension as if it occurred moments ago.

"I was driving to work in my steam craft"—

"Your what?" Michael interrupted.

"The ship we landed here in. I didn't expect your primitive brain to comprehend it," she said with a groan. "Anyway, I was running late for an important meeting, so I took a backroad. That's when our paths crossed."

Alexa looked over at Ursula's trembling face. She remembered the day just as well, nodding along as she spoke.

"She was driving way over the speed limit that fateful day. How she even got to the sixth dimension is beyond me. That woman has probably been dimension jumping her entire life, hoping to find a suitable home."

"And it seems she settled for you," Michael said.

"Not exactly," Alexa replied.

Michael looked at her in confusion. Isabella and Julianna mirrored while Ursula looked the other way.

Alexa took a deep breath. "Just as it was my turn to go through the four way intersection, that moron comes flying in, hitting me on my left side. I swear that imbecile must have never driven in her life."

The memory of their collision still sent her blood boiling. Not as much as it did when it happened. Rather, there was a calmness to that day now.

"I took her to court immediately after that. After just a few minutes, the jury concluded Ursula could not pay for the damages on my steam craft. She had two options left: a life sentence or an execution."

"That seems rather extreme for a traffic offense," Michael suggested.

"Not when it wasn't your first accident," Alexa replied with a stoic glare.

Michael stared in silence, racing with what sort of trouble she caused with past incidents. Julianna and Isabella were just as nervous, turning their attention towards Ursula. She looked away, trembling with fear.

"It also didn't help that any crimes dealt against the queen were handled with extra severity."

Alexa recalled the court hearing and the judge's immediate inclination to favor her. They never so much as glanced over her file. The jury and the audience were all on her side, as well, leaving Ursula to represent herself.

"Seeing the despair in her eyes, I knew I couldn't let her ago. She was an idiot, but no one deserves to go down that way."

She recalled Ursula's whimpering terror and the tears that spilled from her face in the courtroom before the judge.

"What I did was quite controversial. I pleaded to the jury to let me take her in as my servant to pay for my damages. This happened about a year ago. We've been tied at the hip ever since."

Michael only realized now Alexa had smiled during the last part of her story, and he smiled, too. "I understand now."

"You understand what?" said Alexa.

"You really care about that girl, don't you? However, your cruel ways as a tyrannical businesswoman have prevented you from ever showing her the care that she deserves," he said.

"You just like making assumptions, don't you? A narcissistic prick is what you are," Alexa said with a scowl.

"I'm sure you probably had some sort of reputation to uphold. Your kind always does," said Michael, looking over at an embarrassed Isabella.

"Shut up. You don't know me!" Alexa refuted.

"I think I do, Alexa. You've grown cold as a leader. Now, the only way you communicate with Ursula is through your rage. Despite all this, I think that deep down, you're a good person," he said.

"What? After everything you've said to me and everything you've seen me do, you still think I'm a good person?" Alexa said, completely confused.

"Yes. I do." Michael replied in a calming tone. "That day you could have let Ursula die or rot in some prison cell. But you showed compassion, despite her inconveniencing you. Although many years of stepping on people for financial and political gain have hardened you to the point where your heart seldom beats, I'm sure you can express your feelings to Ursula appropriately. A way that shows the compassion I know you have for her."

Tears flowed from Alexa's face. "Damn it! Why did you have to read so much into everything? I was just trying to do something nice for once that day."

"That's how he is." Isabella smiled.

"Kind-hearted and resilient. Even if he is a little stupid sometimes." Julianna smiled, too.

"And while you probably made her life difficult, I'm sure she was grateful to you for allowing her to have one at all," Michael said to Alexa.

He looked over at Ursula and smiled. She looked back at him and smiled back.

"You're right." Alexa began, with a deep breath. "Ursula means a great deal to me. I've just never been able to express myself, as you said."

"It's not too late. I'm sure Ursula's waiting to start the life she wanted all along. A life where she can call you her friend," Michael said.

"A friend."

Alexa dropped to her hands and knees. The titan disappeared, returning the lands to their peaceful state.

Michael walked up to her with a smile. "I'm proud of you, Alexa."

"You're proud of me? Why?" Alexa asked.

"Facing your problems is never easy. And you did it. That's why," Michael replied with an earnest grin.

Alexa looked up at him, bewildered, before breaking out into a chuckle.

"You're peculiar, you know that." Alexa rose to her feet, smiled, and wiped her tears. "All my accomplishments, money, and power, yet you're the first to ever acknowledge the kindness deep within me. You're the only person to ever say they're proud of me." Alexa leaned forward, pulled him into a tight hug, and kissed him on the lips, as tears poured down her face.

His eyes quickly widened with disbelief. The girls looked at them both with expressions of frustration and outrage.

"Surely, this is a joke," Julianna said.

"Afraid not. It appears with his kind heart, she's also smitten with him," Isabella said.

Michael released her from his lips and stared into her eyes with a nervous laugh. "You dimension walkers sure are affectionate once you break through your thick exteriors," he said. She nodded and laughed too.

Ursula ran up to them, hugging Alexa with as much tightness as she could muster and crying with joy. "I've waited so long for this day."

"The wait is finally over. I can finally be the person I wanted to be. Someone you deserve. And it's all thanks to Michael," said Alexa, looking over at him.

Michael returned to his normal form and nodded. "It was nothing. I'm just happy to help."

"Is there any way we can return the favor?" Ursula asked, tugging him by one arm.

He looked down at Ursula's low-cut top, and then his face reddened from embarrassment. "None that I can think of, so don't worry about it."

"Yes, Michael." Alexa wrapped herself around his other arm. "If there is anything we can do, please ask. We will make ourselves of use to you, any way we can."

Michael only noticed now her top was just as revealing. He could almost see the outline of her nipples peering from the top. He gulped and looked the other way.

"It's alright, I'm fine," he said in a high-pitched voice.

Isabella and Julianna stormed toward him, grabbing him

by the legs. "He's mine. Hands off, you pink-haired slut!" said Isabella.

"Slut? I don't think so," Alexa replied. "I'm only trying to return the favor."

"Return the favor without kissing my husband," Isabella demanded.

"He's my husband," Julianna protested.

Julianna and Isabella exchanged scornful looks, unaware they were stretching Michael well beyond the point of comfort.

Alexa looked over at them with a smile. "Admittedly, I was a bit jealous when I saw Ursula kiss him with such ardor. I suppose a part of me wanted to experience a bit of that."

"And what did you think?" Ursula asked.

Alexa smiled. "I think he and I are going to be the best of friends."

"Let go of me, please. All of you." Michael gritted his teeth in discomfort from being pulled in four directions.

Julianna and Isabella looked at one another with stern nods.

"I think the competition for his heart just got stiffer," said Julianna, "Which means something else did."

"I say we call a truce. At least until we know for certain he doesn't harbor any feelings towards either of them," said Isabella.

Julianna looked down and saw a clear bulge under Michael's belt. She rolled her eyes and shook her head. Isabella noticed it too and reacted the same way.

"What a masochist," they both said.

"Well, since you offered a repayment, Alexa, I'd be happy with you teaming up with us. That is, once you and the others put me down."

"You mean that?" Alexa said, wide-eyed.

The four of them placed him back on his feet. He relaxed his muscles back into place while he caught his breath.

"Yeah. We're going after the same organization and, together, we have four titans against their two. We'll be unstoppable!"

"Which means they can never have more than us," Isabella said, smiling with optimism.

"That demon king will be history," Julianna said with a confident smile.

Right, Michael thought, *I got so caught up in dealing with these two I nearly forgot the dream I had with Lucifer.*

He looked around at the smiling faces and nodded.

When I had that vision of something flying down from another world, this was far from what I expected. But I can't complain. With two more allies, we'll be even stronger. I'll be sure to tell all of them my findings once my back stops aching so much.

"This is great," Ursula said in an enthusiastic tone. "The five of us. A total dream team!"

"I'll have some royals ship over necessary funds. A mission like this could take a while," said Alexa.

"I guess we're setting up camp for two more," Julianna suggested.

"We sure are," Michael replied.

They all looked at each other with wide enthusiastic smiles, confident about the new friendship and adventures ahead of them.

CHAPTER 5
THE FACE OF ALL YOUR FEARS

A week had passed since Alexa and Ursula joined Michael's group. They settled in with the team, getting along with one another. Despite the occasional difference, their ambitions to defeat the legion of Morningstar remained aligned.

Julianna rose when the sun's light graced the eastern horizon. She wiped the sleepiness out of her eyes and stepped outside to the sound of birdsong. She had a primary task on her mind this day: to sew and enchant infinity bags for the rest of her team. With that on her mind, she gathered her tools, laid them across the wooden table she engineered for this task, and got to work.

Ursula walked up to her with a curious gaze. "Hey, what do you have going on there?"

"It's the new infinity bags I'm making for you," Julianna replied.

"Yes, she's quite the talented one, isn't she?" Isabella chimed in while wrapping her arm around Isabella.

"That's very flattering, but I need to concentrate. One

wrong stitch and the enchantments won't work," Julianna said as she took Isabella's arm off her.

Isabella pouted. "Fine. Refuse the compliment, now, will you?"

Julianna sighed. "If you want me to teach you how to sew, I can do that another time."

Isabella's face lit up with joy. "That would be great!"

"Do you think you could teach me too? These bags look really cute!" Ursula said.

"I'm glad you think so. I picked the colors myself," Julianna proudly said, focusing on the pink bag meant for Alexa.

Alexa didn't share their sentiments. Her focus was elsewhere, reserving her interest for something worth her while.

Ursula looked at her. "Hey, aren't you excited about the bags too?"

Alexa scoffed. "Not even a little."

"You could at least show some gratitude." Isabella bitterly said.

"It's fine. She's just being bitchy because she likes nothing from this dimension," said Julianna.

"That's not it." Alexa sneered.

"Then, what is it?" Julianna asked.

"Did you have to make them the same colors as our hair?" Alexa inquired.

"Why, do you not like it? I thought they'd be easier to identify that way." Julianna explained, surprised by Alexa's opinion.

"You don't think it's strange? I mean, it's bad enough we're using such outdated technology, but to color coordinate on top of that? Seems a bit much. A little childish if you ask me," Alexa said.

"Tell me what you think," Julianna said with a dim eyed glare.

Ursula said, "Oh, come on! They're super adorable. I bet you'll come to love it," nudging her shoulder.

"Doubtful," Alexa said before she turned away from the group.

"I've been meaning to ask; these enchantments, I mean..." Isabella began.

"Yes?" Julianna replied, looking up from the bag she was working on.

"I hate to be rude, but couldn't you put these enchantments on any bag? Why go through the trouble of making new ones?" she asked.

"It's because only a certain material is compatible with the enchantments. None of our current knapsacks will work, so these will have to do," Julianna replied, tightening the seams on Alexa's bag.

"That's a leather outline, right?" Isabella felt her fingers across the smooth strips across the bag. "Won't that get damaged by the rain or snow?"

Julianna smiled. "It's a magic bag. Equipped to combat any outside resistance. Not even a sword could pierce through one of these."

"A sword? Really? That's so cool. Alexa, how could you say this is lame and shitty?" Ursula said, standing over the table with an innocently expectant smile.

"You called my bags lame and shitty?" Julianna asked, looking at them all with a downhearted glare.

Alexa rolled her eyes, placed her palm on her forehead, and shook her head. "Damn it, Ursula! I told you that in secrecy."

"Whoops, sorry. You should have let me have the last slice of smoked beef last night." Ursula pulled on her lower eyelid with her finger mockingly.

"No one gets in the way of my food and you know that!" Alexa responded.

"You girls certainly have an interesting dynamic going on," Isabella said, laughing. "I'm glad to see you're getting along."

"I wouldn't go that far." Alexa crossed her arms and looked away. She peeked back and forth in Ursula's direction before forming a smile. "But, I suppose things could be worse."

"Yeah, I could have gone hungry!" Ursula said with a gasp.

"Shut up." Alexa nudged her with a smile.

"And done!" Julianna said, finishing the last stitch on the bag. "Perhaps now that it's finished, a certain stuck up queen will change her tune."

"Super cute! Alexa, if you don't want it, can I have it?" Ursula asked, holding her bag in the air.

Alexa snatched it from her hands. "No, it's mine." She clasped it and looked away in embarrassment.

Julianna looked over at her with a smug expression. "So, you do like the bag, don't you?

"No, they're fucking stupid. I just don't like sharing with Ursula. That's all," Alexa claimed, blushing.

"Just say you like the bag. Otherwise, I'll have to give it to Ursula. Or even worse, Michael!" Julianna said, grinning.

Alexa's eyes widened. "You wouldn't!"

"I'm an assassin. I can make anything happen." Julianna reached for the bag. Just before she could, Alexa quickly turned away, guarding the bag against her.

"Fine, I like it," Alexa admitted.

"I'm sorry. What was that?" Julianna said, looking over her shoulder.

"I said the bag's great, alright? It's efficient and fashionable," Alexa assertively replied to the group.

"Good. Now, hand it over so I can enchant it for you," said Julianna. Alexa reluctantly did as she requested.

"Hey, speak of the angel; where is he, anyway?" Isabella asked.

Alexa added, "We should be planning team maneuvers to combat the threat of the demon king and his legion. Where the hell is he?"

"It's only nine, so he's probably still sleeping," Julianna replied before enchanting Alexa's bag.

"That'll be the third morning in a row he's missed sword training lessons, correct?" Ursula asked.

"Yes..." Julianna said, regretfully.

"What a bum." Alexa rolled her eyes and sighed.

"Maybe he'd like a bag, too. Perhaps a gift from a pretty girl will motivate him," Isabella said, grinning as she eyed Julianna.

"Flattery won't work for you," said Julianna.

"As if. I was talking about me delivering the bag. I'll see what he's doing." Isabella walked over to his tent.

"Be careful. A man that age could be doing some very questionable things at this hour," Alexa stated, looking over at his tent.

"Like what?" Ursula asked.

"Like playing with himself," Julianna replied with a mischievous grin.

"What? Why would he do that when he has us?" Ursula asked, flabbergasted.

"Who can say? He's always been reserved about his feelings," Isabella said, sighing.

"Maybe he needs a confidence boost," Ursula replied, heading towards his tent.

"Sorry, but satisfying a man's ego is not my problem. If he doesn't realize what he's got, that's his problem," said Alexa.

"How charming. I'm sure when Michael decides on who to marry, he will keep you in mind," Julianna said with a sarcastic smirk.

Alexa replied, "I should hope so. I'm the oldest, tallest,

smartest, richest, and best looking. Even a nitwit like him would know I'm the obvious choice."

"Hey, guys!" Isabella shouted in their direction from outside his tent. "Come Look!"

"Why, what's wrong?" Julianna asked as she and Alexa rushed towards his tent to join the others.

"I swear. That man needs so much coddling," Alexa said, shaking her head.

"I'm sorry. Wasn't it you who cried in his arms after he beat you?" Julianna said.

"It was a fucking tie, damn it!" said Alexa, her face reddening.

They peeked in Michael's tent and found him lying half-naked in a scatter of empty beer and liquor bottles, reeking of alcohol.

"Disgusting!" Alexa said.

"I knew he was a drinker, but I didn't know it was this bad," said Julianna.

"Wow...that is a lot of drinking. No wonder he can't get up past noon!" Ursula said, amazed at the sheer quantity of bottles in his tent.

"Where does he even get the money? He has no job and we don't give him any," Julianna said.

"He probably pickpockets. Dirty thief!" said Alexa, kicking him in the side. The other girls looked at her in shock.

"Why would you assume that?" Isabella asked with a nervous glance.

"You rule over a land long enough, you can distinguish the crooks from the mere peasants," Alexa insisted.

"You shouldn't kick him over an accusation, though!" Ursula shouted.

"I told you I'm good for the money. Now, I'll get to it when I get to it!" Michael said, tossing and turning.

He creaked his eyes open, feeling an ache in his stomach. He looked around the tent and found the girls looking down at him. They were mortified and dumbfounded, according to the looks on their faces. He took a deep breath, realizing he was no longer dreaming.

"Oh, it's just you guys. I swear, these past nights, all my dreams have been about either me drinking or being chased by weird monsters. Sometimes both," he said, recalling a dream of himself being intoxicated while being chased by demonic clowns.

"Well, maybe if you eased up on your liquor consumption" —

Michael ignored Alexa and instead looked around the tent, glancing at the countless bottles around him.

"Oh, I'm sorry. Let me clean this up."

The bottles clanked as Michael pushed them into the corner. It was as if the movement stirred up the pungent smell. He dusted off the dirt collected under them for the girls to take a seat whenever they wanted to.

Alexa looked at him, lost for words. "You are a curious one, aren't you?"

"Hey, apologize for kicking him!" Julianna said, punching Alexa in the arm.

"I'm sorry I woke you up before noon. I'm a total bitch for that," Alexa replied, filled to the brim with sarcasm and devoid of empathy.

"That was you?" Michael rubbed the sore spot on his stomach. "In that case, would you mind sitting outside? For reasons."

Isabella smirked. "You just got rejected."

"Shut it!" Alexa shouted.

She took a deep breath, struggling to regain her composure before staring back at Michael. "Jokes aside."

"How was kicking me a joke?" Michael asked.

"You should know it's inappropriate to sleep in and *booze* like this. It's bad for your health," Alexa said.

Michael stared blankly at her. "Oh, no worries. My health isn't that important to me. Thanks for your concern, though. I've been thinking of maybe cutting back since money's so tight. People watching out for pickpockets and all."

Michael stood up and kissed her cheek. Alexa looked at him, confused as he made his way out of the tent.

"What the hell was that? I hurt you and you thank me?" Alexa placed her hand on his shoulder.

"Oh, don't get me wrong, I'm still kind of mad about that, but you can make it up to me by buying me beers for the next month. How does that sound?" said Michael.

Alexa looked at him in silence. Not by choice, but because she could muster any words in response. Her eyebrows twitched aggressively.

"If I can be serious for just one moment, there's something problematic about what you just said," Isabella said to Michael

"Yeah. You really don't care about your health?" Ursula's voice broke as she asked with a frown.

"Not really. I sort of just go with the motions. Always have. Given my track record, if I were to get sick or die, I'd probably deserve it," Michael said, nonchalantly.

"That's horrible!" Isabella scowled, then smacked her hand against his cheek. "How can you say such a thing?"

The other girls weren't too pleased with him either, but the look on his face told them he just couldn't see why.

"If you're that concerned about my drinking, I'll try to quit. But not before I cash in on that deal with Alexa, first." He gave her a friendly pat on the head. She snapped and bent his fingers back.

"We're trying to tell you something important, you jackass!"

"She's right. And it's not just your drinking," said Isabella.

"Your attitude, your sleeping habits, your memory... Don't you care about any of this?" Julianna asked.

An indifferent Michael wandered off and rummaged under his pillow to find a whiskey bottle. "What about it all?" Michael replied, guzzling down the whisky.

"Michael, where were you born?" Isabella asked with a dissatisfied look on her face.

"No clue," Michael said, fleeting a look up at her before returning to his drink.

"And when were you born?" Isabella asked.

"Who cares? I'm twenty. I know that much," he replied before finishing his bottle.

"Michael, do you know anything about your past at all?" Isabella pressed on.

Michael tossed the bottle to the side. "What are you getting at here?"

"I think the reason your memory is so bad might have something to do with your drinking," said Isabella. The other girls nodded in agreement.

"Wait, hold on. You're saying I can't remember my days as an archangel because of a couple of bottles of beer?" Michael was both surprised and offended by the accusation.

Isabella sighed. "Look, recovering memories from a past life would be difficult for anyone, but downing all this liquor can't be making this any easier. I think you need to quit."

"And you all feel this way?" Michael looking around the tent, seeing the sincerity in everyone's eyes.

"Sorry, but you're only hurting yourself," said Julianna.

"She's right. Plus, you stink!" Ursula added, covering her nose from the stench of whiskey.

"I know I give you a hard time every once in a while." Alexa stared into his eyes with a warm gaze that left him shaking. "I do that out of love, believe it or not."

"That's a little difficult to believe, considering you didn't save me any dinner last night," said Michael, rolling his eyes.

"Tough decisions needed to be made." Alexa took a deep breath. 'Not the point. What we're trying to say is we love you, Michael, and we want the best for you. Please take care of yourself because you matter to us. All of us." The girls looked at him with expressions of swelling concern.

Michael looked around, overwhelmed with disbelief. "I matter that much to you?"

"Of course you do! We love you. Just like she said," said Ursula.

"And we'll help you uncover your memories once we deal with the titans and the Legion of Morningstar," said Alexa.

Right, Michael thought. *I've been drinking so much lately, I've completely forgotten to tell them I met Lucifer in that dream.*

The memory of Lucifer sitting in his chamber with the crow mask on faded in and out of his jaded mind like shuffled fragments. It took all his strength to stay focused.

Maybe I have a problem, he thought, looking down with remorse.

"Michael?" Isabella tapped his shoulder to assure he was alright amidst his shivering.

Tears rolled down his face. "Alright. I'll try. Any suggestions on where to start?"

"Yeah, start by cleaning your tent. I've seen pigpens that smell better than this," Ursula said, trying not to gag.

"Got it!" Michael gathered the bottles and filled them in a garbage bag, then took them outside. "Now, what?"

Julianna took a deep breath before speaking. "I know of a potions shop nearby. They might have something that can help you quit and recover your memories."

"You're not talking about that place in *Ruksmounth*, are you?" Isabella groaned.

"I know they aren't very friendly towards demons, but it's

the only place you can pick up a potion of this caliber on such short notice."

"Alright, then." Isabella sighed.

"I suppose that works for me," Michael began. "How much is it going to be, though? I don't exactly have a ton of cash to my name."

"That's fine. We'll cover the costs, as long as we see improvement," said Isabella. The other girls nodded.

"Really?" Michael's face lit up with elation. "Thank you."

"You're welcome." Julianna smiled. The rest of the girls nodded and mirrored her smile.

"Then, it's settled. Potions shop, here we come!" Ursula said, raising her fist in the air.

The girls nodded in agreement before they returned to their tent to get dressed for the journey. Meanwhile, Michael scampered to the first pieces of clothing he could find and tossed them on with a smile plastered on his face.

I can't believe they'd go this far to help me. Michael remembered the days of the townspeople ridiculing him. He still very much felt it. But with his companions, the sorrow was a lot less.

I need to do my best to clean up my act. Michael stared at the bags of bottles in his tent. *Not just for myself, but for them.*

Michael tied the laces on his boots and prepared his sword by his side. He closed the zipper on his way out of the tent, leaving behind garbage bags filled with bottles, a pile of his other clothes, his sleeping bag, and a lingering shadow.

The human figure of the shadow peered through the walls of the tent with red eyes, grinning maliciously under the beak of a crow mask.

After around an hour of traveling through the woods, Michael and his friends reached Ruksmounth, a quaint village in the Light Realm with modest architecture and an intimate population of working artisans.

As they continued to walk its dirt tattered streets in search of the potion shop, Michael noticed many passersby looking at him with disgust, some whispering among themselves and looking the other way, and some even running from him.

"Hey, what's the deal with all these people? Is this my doing?" Michael asked.

"Don't worry about them. Those guys are probably just jealous. Not often does a man gets to be around even one girl like us, let alone four," said Julianna.

"Yeah, can't say I blame them. I'd be pretty jealous, too. Not sure if I'd make such lecherous eye contact, though," Michael said, as he noticed all the men looking at the girls with depraved glares.

"You're telling me. It's like they're undressing us with their eyes," Ursula said, shivering with disdain as she clung tightly to Michael and Alexa.

"Just ignore them," Alexa replied.

"Are you sure you're all fine out here, though? Some of these people look super creepy...and dangerous," said Michael, gulping at the towering and hairy men who seemed to be closer rather than further.

"He makes a good point. I warned you of this place. They're probably eyeing us for the slaughter. Perhaps even burn us at the stake," said Isabella.

"Burn us?" Ursula's eyes widened.

"That's a gross exaggeration," Julianna insisted. "We'll all be fine, so long as we stick together and focus on the task at hand."

"Hey, is that the shop?" Ursula said, pointing at a nearby sign.

"Wow, what tipped you off? The potions out front or the sign that fucking says potion shop?" Alexa said, annoyed.

"You don't have to be so mean," Ursula replied, pouting.

"She's right. Let's go!" Michael rushed towards the entrance as the others followed him in.

They walked into the shop, then noticed a well-kept young man in his thirties sitting behind the counter.

"What can I do for you?" the man asked with a warm smile.

"We'd like something that cures memory loss. Also, if you have something that combats a drinking addiction, that would be great," said Isabella.

"Sounds like two sides of the same coin," the man said with a joking smile.

"Do you have it or not?" Alexa asked.

"Don't be rude," Ursula whispered.

"I'm not sure," the man said with a pensive glare. "I'll have to take a look, but we rarely have anything like that in stock."

The man rifled through the shelves behind him before moving towards the ones under the desk. He opened each compartment, checking the flasks and bottles within each one, but found nothing.

"Doesn't look like we have it. Apologies." The man looked up with a smile.

Alexa scowled. "Money is no object and we plan on becoming regular buyers of said potions."

The man's face lit up. "In that case, I think there might be something in the back."

"Excellent. See to it that these potions meet our exact needs," said Julianna.

"Oh, that won't be a problem. No problem at all."

The man entered the back room and closed the door behind him. Michael and the girls looked at each other, shrugging off his peculiar behavior as they waited for him to return with the potion.

HE NAVIGATED THROUGH AN ISLE OF SHELVES AND PUSHED another door that led him into a dust-ridden room with several men seated around a table. The table had a scatter of cards, gold, and blades.

"Hey, it's that pretty boy with the white hair," said the man from the counter.

"You mean the guy with those two girls?" The man nearest to him placed his cards down beside his dagger and pile of silver coins. "Didn't he learn his lesson the last time we chased him out?"

"Apparently not," the first man began. "Because this time, he has four girls. All of which are demons."

Their eyes widened. They sprang up from their chairs. The scratching of wood against the stone floor filled the room.

"Is this some sort of joke? Doesn't that fool realize how offensive this behavior is in the church's name?" another of the men asked.

"Dark lovers," the largest man at the table grunted under his breath. "Cretans from the enemy realm. And a fellow light lover. To think one of our own would betray us in such a manner. In the church's presence."

"What should we do?" the man half his size beside him asked with a squeaky tone of voice.

"At this rate, he'll ruin Ruksmounth's reputation as one of the light realm's holiest cities," said another man.

"Not unless we dispose of him. That just takes the right potion," the first man began.

The other men looked at one another. Nefarious grins formed across their faces.

"So, what sort of potion do you think will do the trick? How best can we teach this kid those demons don't belong here?" another man inquired.

The first man grinned and grabbed a blackened potion from the top shelf. "You just leave that to me."

☙❦

MICHAEL AND THE GIRLS HELPED THEMSELVES TO THE SEATS in the shop. Michael sighed as the minutes continued to pass without a sign of the shop owner.

"What's taking so long?"

"Who knows? I just hope he's got something that can help you," said Ursula.

"As do I." Michael nodded.

The door then opened, and the man came back holding a black potion in his hand. "My apologies. Here's your potion, as requested. It retrieves memories and helps combat addiction. A rare specimen. Usually two hundred gold, but for you, I'll do one hundred and fifty."

"Rather pricey, but if it's a two in one, sure," Isabella replied, putting the money on the counter.

"Great! Thanks for doing business with me," the man said.

"Thank you!" Ursula replied, waving as they walked out of the shop.

Fools. The man thought, snickering.

The sun began to set as the five of them completed their journey back to their campsite. Michael looked down at the bottle in his hands. The dark-colored brooding miasma seeping from the top gave him a sinking feeling.

"So, are you going to try it out?" asked Alexa.

"Yes, that was expensive, so it better work," Isabella said.

"Alright. I'll give it a try," Michael agreed.

Michael took a deep breath and then swallowed a heavy gulp from the bottle. He waited a moment for the effects to kick in. He stood there in silence, staring at the bottle with relief. Confusion and disappointment seeped in.

"I guess it doesn't work. Sorry."

"Are you serious? You don't feel anything at all?" Isabella asked.

"Nothing," Michael replied.

"Maybe you need to drink the entire thing for it to work," Ursula suggested.

"Yes, that man was oddly unspecific regarding the proper intake," said Julianna.

"Do you think it'll be fine?" he asked.

"What do you think will happen?" Isabella asked back. Cold sweat rolled down her neck.

Michael looked down at the bottle again. He swore he could see something festering within...screaming at him.

I need to do this, he said to himself. *I need to get better. Otherwise, I won't be the person I need to be for them. Or able to stop Lucifer.*

He confidently nodded before downing the rest of the bottle. He waited, letting the rest of the bottle sink in. Still, he felt no change at all.

"That's strange. I still can't feel anything"—

A sudden pain spread across his body. He grunted helplessly before storming off to his tent, swiftly shutting himself in.

"Michael, are you alright?" Isabella asked, standing outside of the tent.

"I'm fine, I mean, I'm fine," said Michael, in a series of unusual voices.

"You don't sound fine. Let me see what's going on," Alexa said, as she unzipped the tent entrance. The girls froze in shock. Michael had transformed into a woman!

"Unholy shit!" said Ursula.

Michael covered himself up with a handful of blankets, embarrassed.

"Don't look at me," he announced, trying to disguise his

new feminine tonality with a masculine undertone. His mind struggled to wrap around what was happening to him. That, plus the girls talking over each other, turned his panic into a meltdown.

"Your face. Your hair. Are those boobs?" Julianna asked, getting a closer look.

Tears rolled down his face as his transformation became too much to handle.

"That fucking snake of a salesman," said Alexa.

"He's kind of cute, though, if that helps," Ursula commented on Michael's new state.

"That's not the point," said Alexa.

"Sorry." Ursula whimpered with a downhearted glare.

"This is unacceptable what happened. We're marching back to that shop right now. And Michael, you're coming with us."

"I can't!" said Michael, covering his face with his now much longer hair.

"You can and you will!" said Alexa.

"But, why do you need me? I'm sure they already know they gave me this potion to take. It was probably out of spite," said Michael.

"Exactly. That is why we want you to come along. We want them to see what that little joke of theirs did to you and we want you to see what happens to people who get on our wrong side," Alexa said, grinning.

Michael reluctantly nodded.

"Oh, but you can't wear that," Isabella said, referring to the outfit he put on.

"Why not?" Michael said, confused.

"Because it's too boyish. You need more ladylike clothing like dresses and skirts and jewelry," said Isabella.

"Don't force him. This is already difficult enough for him," said Alexa.

"I knew the church fancied degrading people, but their belief that turning a man into a woman is supposed to be some sort of trick is offensive on countless levels. I'm not even sure where to begin." Julianna's face turned as red as her hair.

"It's alright," Michael began.

Their eyes widened in unison.

"Are you sure? You really don't have"—

"I don't mind." Michael took a deep breath. "Those people can insult me all they want, but I won't let them pull such a tasteless prank and get the last laugh."

Julianna smiled. "Good. Let's be on our way soon then."

"You get him changed and we'll get our things ready," said Alexa.

"Got it!" said Isabella.

The girls walked out of the tent. Michael tossed and turned as Isabella helped him get dressed.

Isabella stepped out of the tent and said, "We're all done!" The girls looked back around, curious to see what she had prepared for him. "Come on out."

With a nervous gulp, Michael shambled out of the tent. He stood in front of them in a long flowing white dress with a small gold necklace and earrings to match, and slippers. He looked the other way, brushing the hair out of his face. The girls looked at him, wide-eyed.

"Meet Michelle. A simple artisan who seeks to make it big in the light realm by sewing handbags. What do you think?" said Isabella.

"I think it'll do," Alexa said with a smile.

"...and may I say; I'm impressed by your openness to the idea," Julianna said.

"Well, I didn't expect I'd be wearing something this feminine." Michael blushed, feeling the outlines of his undergarments press under his dress.

"You look beautiful!" Ursula commented.

"You think so?" Michael asked.

"Yes, you're very pretty. Now, let's go." Alexa placed her hand on his back and gave him a gentle push to get going. The rest of the girls followed. With a blush, Michael nodded and started the walk, determined to face the man who played the trick on him.

The leering men on the village streets only made Michael feel worse this time.

"These creepy looks are so much worse when they're directed at me. I have no idea how you girls do it."

"You're about to see how," Julianna said as they walked back into the potion shop. "You, sir!" She pointed directly at the man at the counter.

The man looked up with amusement. The look on his face silently screamed, 'It worked!' He asked, "Something I can help you with?"

Julianna ran up to the counter and grabbed him by the tie of his vest. She slammed his face against the wooden table, scattering blood from his mouth. The whimpering man looked up at her in horror.

"Don't get fucking smart with me. You just couldn't handle the fact that our friend associates himself with demons, now could you?" Juliann shouted, "So, you turned him into a woman. For what? To get a good laugh? Well, the joke's on you!"

Julianna looked at the terrified salesperson. "Now, you're going to give me an antidote and a refund or I'll burn this fucking place to the ground."

The man grinned. "Make your threats. Even if you dare to follow through, a woman like you would never last in prison."

Julianna scoffed with derision. "That's assuming they can catch me."

The man looked at her, wide-eyed.

She turned around at the group. "Everyone, get out, or burn alive!" Michael and the girls scampered out of the shop. The occasional patron joined them in exit while most others in the shop hanged around with doubtful looks on their faces.

"You're bluffing!" said the man.

"Assassins don't bluff about these sorts of things. It's your funeral," Julianna said, grinning.

A harsh orange glow broke in through the window along with the smell of smoke. A crackling sound caught the man's attention as the fire began catching from the canopy outside the shop.

"What's this?"

He walked towards the flame to investigate. The fire spread to the walls and ceiling too. The remaining patrons rushed out with screams of terror.

This can't be, he thought. *Those damn demons.*

The inferno grew into chaos, claiming everything in its way as it traveled onto the bookshop and wand shop on either side.

Julianna walked through the debris, unscratched, hurling gas lamps to feed the fire on her way out.

"Not very subtle for an assassin." Alexa looked around, watching the city collapse under the fire of Julianna's vendetta.

"There'll be no evidence once the bodies are burned to ash," Julianna replied.

She then handed Michael a potion.

"Take this."

"What is it?" Michael asked.

"It's a nullify potion. As it suggests, it undoes any potion you took within the last twenty-four hours," said Julianna.

"That's gotta be expensive!" said Michael.

"Yes, usually five hundred gold. This one's on me. Well, technically on the store, since I stole it at the last second,"

Julianna said, as the fire burst in size, roaring as the melted flesh of the shop owner peered through the crumbled wood remains.

"Glad I'm not that bastard." Michael thought.

The potions within the shop spilled from their shattered casings, forming pools of runoff in the alleyways. Slowly, the effects of all the potions from the shop began to take effect on the village: humans turned to frogs, water turned to blood, what remained of the townspeople killed each other in a psychotic rage, and the village became plagued with cattle and bears. All this while fire and ice rained from the sky.

Michael and the girls marveled at the disarray filling the streets. They huddled up to shield themselves from getting infected.

"One more thing. You should take it when you get home," said Julianna.

A mess of giant black-bear-wolf hybrids covered in blood ran through the town. Flying books, blades, and other objects followed, each coming from various directions, as minuscule vegetation protruded from the ground.

"Sounds like a plan," Michael said, noticing his skin turn purple and green as boils formed on it. The side effects of the many potions spilling through the streets sank in. His heart thundered out of control.

"Let's make it quick before he gets worse," said Isabella.

The group ran back to their campsite, arriving just as the moon began to hang in the sky by itself, leaving the village in its carnivalesque and catastrophic state behind.

Thirty minutes passed before they sat around the table, looking at the strangest Michael they'd ever seen: morphed skin, a whole different gender, and animal-like features.

"Whenever you're ready, Michael," Ursula said.

"I'm not sure I can reach," he replied through swollen

cheeks, as the thick boils and fur around his arms kept his arms from bending towards him.

"Apologies. Let me help."

Julianna emptied the flask down Michael's mouth. A massive burst of light covered him the moment Michael gulped the last of it, blinding the girls for a moment before revealing him in his original state.

"You're back!" Isabella said before jumping into a tight embrace with him. "And you're still wearing those clothes."

"I'll be sure to change. Into my old clothes, I mean," Michael said with a nervous laugh. "Though, I must say; they're rather comfortable. Rather, they were when my body better fit them."

He crossed his legs with embarrassment.

"You really are strange." Ursula laughed.

"Coming from someone who sniffs people," said Julianna.

"It's how we say hello in the first dimension," Ursula insisted.

"That aside, it's strange none of us were affected by any other potions," said Isabella.

"I've heard rumors of a potion on the black market that absorbs the effects of any other potions once someone drinks it. It prevents any others from getting ill. They call it the black sheep potion," said Julianna.

"How fitting for me." Michael smiled.

"I'm glad you're feeling better," Said Ursula. "And that you're able to keep that sense of humor through all this."

"Of course. So long as I've got you guys and the shop owner is burning away, what is there to be bitter about?" Michael replied.

The girls shared a laugh.

"Feeling ready to quit drinking and focus on regaining your memories now?" Alexa asked.

Michael looked back at the four of them and smiled back.

J.J. EGOSI

"I sure am."

CHAPTER 6
DRAGGED DOWN MEMORY LANE

An expanse of darkness surrounded Michael. It was devoid of sound, but for the howling wind past him and his heightened heartbeat. Michael looked around the entrapment of endless blackness. He waved his hand forward to ensure there were no obstacles and took a cautious step forward before walking on. He moved aimlessly into what seemed to be eternal nothingness when the sound of disembodied murmurs faded into his ears.

"Become the real *you*," a voice whispered.

"Leave this *you* behind and embrace the true *you*," said another voice.

The haunting whispers with a common message grew into torturous distortion. Michael didn't even realize his cautious walk had turned into a frenzied sprint for his safety, fighting to escape the torturing howls in his mind.

"Shut up. I have no idea what you're talking about. I'm *me*. Michael. That's it." He covered his ears as he ran, hoping to block out the voices.

"No, Michael. You're not who you think you are, but another person, entirely," said another voice.

"I have no idea what that even means. Fuck off! Just leave me alone!" Michael shouted.

He stopped in his tracks, met now by a materializing shadow of demonic faces. They grinned maliciously from every direction, like a prison with no escape.

"Embrace yourself, Michael. For it is only through reconciliation that you may find any salvation."

"Damn it. Just shut up," Michael screamed as he fell to his knees.

"Hey, Michael? Earth to Michael?" said Ursula.

He suddenly realized someone was calling out to him and he turned around, only to find himself far from any dream. The world around him had now transformed into a woodland where he saw Ursula and the other girls.

"Hey, are you alright?" Ursula asked.

"Yeah, sorry. I guess I got lost in my thoughts," said Michael, realizing he'd dozed off again. He took a sigh of relief.

She and the other girls looked at him with visible concern as they continued walking through the forest in search of firewood.

"You seem to daydream a lot these days," said Isabella.

"Yeah, things have been a bit weird for me, lately. I guess it's because I haven't been drinking anymore," Michael said, collecting his thoughts.

"I know things can't be easy for you now, but we're proud of you. You've gone a whole week without drinking and we'd like to celebrate with a bonfire tonight," Julianna said, resting her hand on his shoulder.

He looked over at her and smiled. "Thanks. I appreciate it."

"No problem at all," she said, smiling back.

"Anyway, do you guys have any idea what you want to eat tonight?" Alexa asked.

"Oh, I have an idea," Julianna said, snickering.

"Really? What did you have in mind?" Unamused, Michael looked at her. He knew exactly what she was going to say.

"How about a nice roasted black bear," Julianna said with a laugh. Isabella joined in on the laughter.

"What's so funny?" Ursula inquired as she and Alexa looked at them, confused. Isabella and Julianna whispered something in their ears. Michael didn't have to hear it to know they were talking about his history with black bears. The girls looked at him and giggled.

"Hilarious, guys. I told you that in secrecy. And for the record, that baby bear was way stronger than it led on," said Michael. The girls burst out with laughter as they pointed at him. "It's not that funny, guys."

As Alexa's laughter dwindled, she placed her hand on his shoulder, hoping to say something that could distract her from the amusement that coursed through her. She succumbed to even more laughter that she could do nothing about.

"I preferred when we were talking about my drinking problems," Michael muttered to himself.

"Alright, I'm sorry. But if it's true a couple of bears beat you, you and I have to battle again. I can't allow myself to share in your shame," said Alexa.

"Glad to know you're worried about how I feel," Michael said with a dim-eyed glare. "Although, a rematch isn't all that important at the moment."

"Unless you want to get your ass kicked for a second time." Julianna snickered.

"Do you want to get your ass kicked?" Alexa tightened her hand into her fist with eyes flaring in Julianna's direction.

"Michael's right," Isabella began, "We've got bigger things to worry about, like preparing a counterstrike against the legion of Morningstar."

Michael gulped, remembering he still hadn't told them.

"That's a good point. We have no clue when they may strike. Though with four titans against their two, we should be fine," said Ursula.

"Just in case though, we should recruit some extra teammates. Maybe some black bears," said Isabella.

She and the girls burst into laughter again. It didn't bother Michael this time as he drowned in guilt and fear for not disclosing his encounter with Lucifer yet.

Why haven't I told them? Am I afraid?

He could only recall the demonic faces from his previous dream. He shuddered at the memory of them. He couldn't take it any longer. When he turned towards the girls, their faces morphed into the very faces in his dream.

"Michael?" Isabella asked.

"Hey, we're sorry. We'll stop making fun of you. Really," said Julianna.

His vision faded. His breathing heightened as he prepared to storm into the woods, as far away from them as possible.

"Just where do you think you're going?"

Michael's heart raced as the grip of his nightmares took hold. He looked over his shoulder, seeing Alexa's worry-ridden face. His breathing slowly calmed.

"Just what's your deal? Are you really that enamored by a silly joke you'd try running away like a child?"

Michael looked at their faces, seeing they had returned to normal He took a deep breath and smiled.

"My apologies. I'll try to build thicker skin," he said.

...and hopefully, fast. I can't keep hiding this secret from them forever.

"No, I think we should just try to refrain from teasing you. Funny as it is." Ursula covered the snicker coming from her mouth.

"Don't worry about it," Michael replied in a startled state.

"Besides, we're making terrible progress with wood collecting."

"Well, that's because you're hardly contributing," Ursula said, looking at the lone twig in his hand. The rest of the girls laughed.

"Yeah, is that all you can carry?" Alexa said, annoyed.

"Maybe all the whiskey numbed his muscles?" Ursula suggested.

"That makes no sense," Julianna replied.

"Clearly, you've never been drunk," Ursula said with a grin.

Michael only realized how much wood the girls carried. Each of them held considerable amounts of logs on their shoulders. He looked down at the single twig in his hand and frowned, realizing he'd allowed his nightmares to distract him.

"Sorry. I guess the wood collecting got away from me with all my dozing off."

"Oh, don't worry about it," Ursula said, smiling.

"Really. To thank you for the other day, let me take care of the wood. I'll even handle the hunting," Michael said.

"You? Hunting?" Isabella smirked.

"I think you mean getting hunted," Julianna joked.

"You walked into that one, I'm afraid." Alexa laughed.

Michael groaned. "Laugh all you want, but I'm serious."

"Michael, do you have any idea what you're even saying? You can't handle wood collecting and hunting on your own. Even with all of us, it could take hours upon hours," said Isabella.

Michael smiled. "Perhaps that was true before. Now that I've realized my abilities as the archangel, I think I can get it done in five minutes."

"That's rather arrogant," said Alexa.

"Like you have any room to talk," Isabella said.

"Just get your infinity bags ready, everyone," Michael said with finality.

The girls looked at him in confusion, shrugging his comment off. Michael transformed into his angel form. He materialized his scepter in his hands, bringing a burst of wind with him. The girls watched him in awe and shock.

"You realize magic is outlawed in the twilight realm now because of recent bans placed from the village we destroyed, right?" Alexa said.

"A quick spell won't hurt anyone, right?" said Michael.

The skies filled with lightning strikes. The winds grew intense as the animals flocked for safety.

"Why not? Fuck the church, I suppose," Alexa said. The others nodded.

With a smile, he held up his scepter and pointed it at the trees. "Light beam slash!"

With outward curve-like slashes, he cut every tree in front of himself and the girls down to size, leaving the logs laid out in neat stacks.

Michael then turned around. "There. Now, it's time for the hunt."

The girls marveled at the neat stack of logs before watching Michael fly into a part of the woods that was unaffected by his spell. He rustled past the trees as he disappeared into the thicket, leaving the girls waiting eagerly. The sound of roars and squeals from the direction he went stopped before Michael returned with slaughtered bears and hogs in his hands.

"Alright, this should be enough food and wood for a few months. Let's say we get this all in those bags of yours and head out!" said Michael.

His display left the girls lost for words. They simply nodded in acknowledgment.

As the five of them walked over to their campsite, Alexa

looked around at the group. "So, with the five of us teamed up now, does anyone have any plans on how to defeat the Legion of Morningstar?"

"A battle between two titans could prove dangerous. And we have no clue what the demon king is capable of," said Isabella.

"Indeed. And let's not forget that their leader has business with Michael," said Julianna, looking at Michael.

Michael nervously laughed with a nod.

"Well, their leader will never take us down!" said Ursula.

"Hey, I've been meaning to ask you something..." Isabella started.

"Yeah, what?" Ursula wondered as everyone looked at her with curiosity.

"That day you fought Michael. Your eyes. They turned black. What was that all about?" said Isabella.

Ursula looked at her. Her cheeks turned rosy in embarrassment. "Oh, right. I've been trying to reach this thing called 'etheria'. Something about conquering your inner demons. I don't know. The whole idea seems really offensive to our kind. It hasn't been going too well so far."

"Oh, I see. I ask because I recently reached a similar state, only I had horns and a tail." Her response earned her stunned looks.

"Sounds like you fully reached the form. Very impressive. I can see how you won your titan ring now," said Alexa. "Perhaps once I trounce Michael and his army of cub scouts, I'll see you on the battlefield."

"Maybe you will," Isabella said with a proud smile.

"Etheria? Interesting. So, you know of it in other dimensions?" Michael asked.

"We sure do. It's the legendary state of demonkind," Ursula said.

"What else do you guys know about it?" Michael asked.

"I think everyone interprets the form a bit differently but I believe etheria is a state achieved by reaching inner peace with oneself..."

Peace with oneself? Michael thought.

"...that's only a part of it. Knowing your purpose and focusing on your endeavors is another part—qualities that Ursula lacks, which is why she still can't power up," Alexa said, looking at a saddened Ursula.

Michael flashed a comforting smile at Ursula and said, "Cheer up. I'm sure you'll get there soon."

"And what is the significance of this state, if you don't mind my asking?" asked Julianna.

"I would think a fellow demon would know that. Maybe the form isn't so well known here in the dark ages, but if you're a dimension walker, everyone knows it as the ultimate prestige of a demon. Only the greatest can reach this form," said Alexa.

Isabella blushed, before meeting the frustrated and envious look on Julianna's face.

"Oh, don't feel so bad, Julianna. You're plenty strong," Michael said, placing his hand on her shoulder.

"Yes, but I want to be stronger. A demon never settles for anything below the highest tier. That's how we've evolved to the highest echelons of beauty, power, and wealth over the years. We strive for perfection and if we can't reach it, then we're failures," said Julianna.

"That's pretty harsh. Well, this probably doesn't mean much, but I don't think you're a failure," Michael assured.

"You don't?" Julianna asked with an expectant look.

"Of course not! You have a successful sword business and a great job as an assassin, to boot. You're great at what you do and, if I may be so bold, you surround yourself with equally great people. You're a total success, as far as I'm concerned," said Michael.

Julianna took a moment to absorb the compliments. She blushed before kissing him on the cheek. Michael returned the sentiment with a smile.

"Now, let's hurry. It's getting dark and we've hardly enough time before the bears I didn't kill come back out," Michael said.

The girls snickered, leaving him groaning with the very thought as they all continued walking with their wood and their bounty of food.

The group returned to the campsite and immediately got to work, constructing a fire pit out of stray stones. The atmosphere brimmed with laughter and smiles as they teamed up to build the bonfire. Once they ignited the fire, they gathered around it and watched the mesmerizing glow of the dancing inferno in the night.

"Hey, Michael..." started Alexa.

"Yeah?" he replied.

"...how'd you do it?"

"How'd I do what?"

"From everything I've heard; you came from nothing. You were beaten to near-death every day and drove yourself into heavy drinking, and yet you have such a positive outlook on life and the people around you. How do you do something like that?" she asked, as the other girls looked at him, curious for an answer as well.

"I don't know. I guess I never got a lot from life but wanted to change that, one day. Life hasn't been very kind to me, but it hasn't stopped me from striving for more. And you know, some days are better. I'd often get depressed until I'd drink myself into a coma," said Michael.

The girls looked at him with frowns and tears forming in their eyes.

"But even on my darkest days, I never lost sight of the light waiting for me. I knew I'd achieve something one day.

I didn't know how, but I just knew. And with the four of you, well, I see people who have made something of themselves. Billion-gold empires in a world that discriminates against your kind. That sense of feeling like a pariah is something I share in. And seeing your success makes me think anything can happen for me if I work hard enough. You're all so inspiring. I don't know what I'd do without you."

"Oh, Michael." Isabella smiled.

"Maybe it's childish envy or whatever. I just know there are great things out there and that no matter what my mind tells me, my heart says it's out there waiting for me," Michael said with a wholesome smile.

The girls smiled in response to his words. "All the money we could ask for, and I think it's you who could teach us a lesson," said Julianna.

"Well, I don't know about that. I think there's plenty I could learn from you. Making money, for one. But, also caring a bit more about myself," Michael said with an awkward laugh.

"Which is what I think you need," said Ursula.

"Making money is easy. Being happy isn't. I know you're used to throwing your health down the drain, but there are people who care about you now, so you'll need to pay attention to the way you treat yourself," said Isabella.

"In other words, you have something to live for. Something to drive you towards that extravagant life of purpose and opportunity you desire so much," said Julianna.

Alexa commented, "Well, if that isn't the truth, I don't know what is," wrapping her arm around his.

Michael smiled. "Thanks, guys."

"Don't thank us. Thank you for your honesty," Ursula said, matching Alexa's grip on Michael's other arm.

"My pleasure," Michael said, blushing.

Michael and the girls watched the fire lose its vigor as dinner ended.

He stared with wonder in his eyes and a smile across his face, imagining the world ahead of him—a life of wealth and opportunity with his friends all by his side.

A goal for me to strive for, he thought. *I'll make that dream a reality and wash away the nightmares.*

A strong wind snuffed the hypnotic flame. Everyone looked up and around the campsite, looking for the source of the unusual weather. As the winds grew aggressive, the group's collective confusion turned into panic.

"What's going on?" Ursula asked.

"Your guess is as good as mine," said Julianna.

A thick blanket of shadows slowly enfolded the moon, twisting and turning as the screaming winds echoed from every corner.

"Some kind of freak storm, you think?" said Isabella.

"I think not," a strange voice responded.

"Who's there?" Alexa said, scanning her surroundings for the source of the voice.

"That voice? It can't be," said Michael.

"Oh, it is," the voice replied, as a great crow circled the tree line, descending gracefully towards them.

"A bird?" Isabella said, confused.

"That's not a bird," said Michael.

"How right, you are!" the voice replied.

The crow landed before them, staring with a chilling set of crimson eyes, before transforming into the masked demon of Michael's nightmares: an imposing man whose blackened aura chilled the once warm air, plaguing it with his dark miasma.

"Who are you?" Julianna said, panicking.

"You don't recognize me? My feelings are hurt. I thought a demon such as myself would be known across all the omniverse, especially to those seeking my titan rings," said the man.

"Omniverse? Titan rings? Are you?"

"That's right," the man said in response to Alexa's questions. "I am the leader of the Legion of Morningstar and I have come for your titan rings, and the man you harbor."

"Yeah, well, you can't have them," Isabella refuted. "Not the rings and not him."

Julianna lowered her voice to say, "Isabella, I don't think you want to mess with this guy; this is the demon king we're talking about. Legend says he's wielded the strongest armies the world has ever known. Some say he's the only demon the church truly fears."

Michael looked at the man, completely mortified, as all color left his face. The girls directed their looks at him.

"Michael, are you alright? You looked incredibly pale," said Julianna.

Alexa waved her hand in his face and nudged him. "Michael? Michael?!" Said Alexa. He simply stared on, fixated by the figure before him.

He thought, *the demon king in my nightmares. Lucifer.*

"I'll take your collective cluelessness as a sign that he hasn't told you about me," said the man.

"Wait, what? Are you saying Michael knows you?" said Julianna.

"That could explain why he's after you if you had a previous run-in," Alexa suggested, gazing at the man's strange mask.

"That's preposterous!" Isabella said. "Michael had never even left the dark realm before the past week or so. There's no way he could have met someone like you without my knowledge about it."

"Though he is the archangel, they're said to know each other well ... And be bitter rivals," said Ursula.

"I know all that. I'm asking if Michael can recognize this plague doctor looking freak right now," Isabella said.

"There's one way to answer that." A devious smiled formed across the man's face. "Ask him if he knows my name."

Isabella gulped as she turned towards Michael. The rest of the girls met him with tense gazes.

"Well?" Ursula asked. "Do you remember his name at all?"

Sweat rolled down his face. The grin on the demon king's face trapped him just as those faces did in his nightmares. There was nowhere to go. He had to confess what he'd been hiding right there and now.

"It's true," said Michael, trembling. "He's the demon that's been haunting my nightmares. His name is Lucifer."

The girls gasped.

"You're joking! You mean you've met him in your night-mares?" Julianna asked.

"Why the fuck didn't you tell us this before?" Alexa demanded.

"I'm sorry. I just"—

"A pity," Lucifer began, "to think your own species would bring such horror to the same man you love. Oh, how you all must be drowning in self-doubt, wondering if you can trust him any longer. He is a liar, after all."

"I didn't lie," Michael appealed. "I just didn't tell."

He looked over at them with a nervous smile. Their stony gazes silently communicated a loss of trust and disbelief in what they had just found out.

"I'm curious if he ever has nightmares about any of you ladies," Lucifer said. "It's not good for an angel to spend so much time with demons after all. In fact, it's rather bad for their health!"

"Do we scare you, Michael? Tell us," Isabella said, trembling with worry, as the other girls looked at him, painfully awaiting his response.

"What's going on? Of course, you don't. You're my"—

He saw their faces contort to those he saw in his night-mares. Gasping, he trembled back. The four of them looked with despair.

"So, you are afraid?" Ursula whimpered, on the verge of tears.

Michael gritted his teeth. To his right, he heard Lucifer's chuckling filling the forest. His blood boiled at the sound as he darted his head towards them.

"That's enough! Stop trying to poison their minds. You know all my recent nightmares were your doing."

"I suppose some tragedies are inevitable. And some night-mares won't go away," Lucifer said.

"And what does that mean?" Michael asked.

"Tell me. What are you most afraid of?" Lucifer asked.

Michael gulped. He trembled in the wake of a grin more terrifying than any he'd ever seen as the hideous miasma spread under Lucifer's mask.

"It's solitude, isn't it?" Lucifer asked.

"How did you"—

"You can't stand the thought of being abandoned. Forgotten by the world. Or as I might say, being left all alone."

Michael's eyes widened. The uncertainty he felt during his prior encounter with Lucifer became clearer, leaving him mortified.

"Your voice. I know where I've heard it." He pieced together the fact that the voice he heard in the twilight forest, haunting his mind, and Lucifer's were the same. "This can't be. This must be a mistake."

"Oh, but it isn't," Lucifer said. "I've been in your mind all along. Watching. Observing what it is you admire most. And what leaves your nightmares running amok? And when it comes to being left behind, that's a nightmare you can't outrun."

"Shut your mouth. I'm"—

"Don't believe me? Look at your friends," Lucifer said.

Michael turned towards the girls and met their wary gazes as they struggled to maintain eye contact with him.

"You want nothing more than to be revered. Loved. Surrounded by those you cherish. Yet, you drive those same people away. How serendipitous."

"That is not true." Michael shivered as he stumbled back. He nearly tripped over his ankle as the dread in his mind took a strangling hold.

Lucifer snickered. "Your dreams were more than just dreams. They were visions. Visions of the future."

"The future?" Michael said, confused.

"Yes, vague as they were, each dream tells a story. Would you care to know a dream of mine?" Lucifer asked.

"As a matter of fact, I wouldn't," Michael said with a scornful glare.

"Well, I'll tell you, anyway, since I'm feeling chatty." Lucifer grinned. "The dream I had was quite real, for it told of something that took place long ago."

"I didn't ask for a history lesson, either," Michael snapped.

"Oh, but it's such a delightful story, Michael," he insisted. "A story depicting the great struggle between two beings that fought against one another for this omniverse countless eons ago. The creator god, Michael, and the destroyer god, Lucifer."

The beating of Michael's heart sped up at the mention of his name. He was certain the association with divinity was a mistake. He was anything but.

Lucifer stared into his panic-induced eyes with a smile.

"That was no mistake. You're that creator and I am that destroyer."

"Did you just say I'm a god? And an archangel?"

"Yes. You were born a god, as I was, and earned the title of archangel through your divine abilities. Just as I earned the title of demon king with my diabolic persuasion," Lucifer replied with a grin.

Michael's head swirled with confusion. His mind overloaded with images he couldn't recognize—eras he'd never experienced, where creatures he'd never witnessed took form, and civilizations he had no recollection of rose and fell. Many worlds dawned and set before his eyes. An immediate bond he couldn't comprehend took hold of him. He couldn't see anything else. All he could see were those visions. And all he could feel was his heart pounding out of his chest.

"That's correct." Lucifer grinned. "The god of creation. The man who birthed this world. And I, the god of destruction, will be the one to take it away."

"Get the fuck out of here. Michael's seriously a god," Ursula said.

"Unholy shit!" Alexa nervously gulped.

Michael turned towards the girls, sensing apprehension building in them as they slowly backed off from him.

"That, I didn't know. I promise."

"Well, it seems my servant, Hecate, did a better job than I expected of not disclosing that information to you," Lucifer began, "I never thought that obsessive little runt could shut her fucking mouth."

Michael gritted his teeth and shifted towards his direction. "She died in your name. Perhaps you could learn something from her sacrifice!"

"Oh, but I'm only here to teach"—Lucifer walked towards Michael with a callous look—"And shed a little enlightenment here. Perhaps you could learn something. A certain sheet of wool over the eyes that needs pulling, yes?"

Michael clenched his fists and turned towards the girls one more time. "Please ... I'm sorry for not telling you earlier. One thing led to another and between my constant drinking, I was never able to do so."

"We heard what you said, Michael," said Ursula. "And we heard what Lucifer said, too."

Lucifer's eyes widened with intrigue.

"Are you really a god?" Isabella asked.

"That, he is," Lucifer replied. "One of the most powerful and ancient there is. Save for yours truly, of course."

"You knew this all along. Why tell us now? Why didn't you have Hecate reveal his nature?" Julianna insisted.

"Oh, no special reason. I just wanted to see the look on all your faces when I told you myself. Especially Michael's," Lucifer replied with a devious grin.

What a bastard, Isabella thought, clenching her fists.

They don't seem as bothered as before, Michael thought, staring at their blank expressions. *Maybe they've forgiven me?*

"Well, we should get down to business. The battle between the two greatest forces is about to begin. I hope your friends have a stronger shelter than those pathetic tents. Otherwise, they'll be blown out of this dimension within seconds," said Lucifer.

The girls backed off as Michael and Lucifer prepared to face off. Michael was done feeding Lucifer's ego by showing fear. He would not back down this time. He kept his eyes pinned into Lucifer's, ready for whatever games he would throw at him.

"This is insane, isn't it? Tell me I'm not the only one that's thinking this," said Isabella.

"You're not. I just can't believe it's true," Julianna said. "The archangel is also the god of creation."

"And given the demon's reputation for his sharp honesty, there's no denying it," said Ursula.

"I knew he was important, but to be the one who created the entire world? I thought that was just a legend," said Alexa.

"Our Michael? The god of all creation?" Isabella said in amazement.

"And the leader of the organization is the god of destruction. How could we have missed that?" Ursula added.

"I don't know, but it looks like hell's about to break, so we should definitely take cover," said Isabella.

"Shouldn't we help him?" Ursula suggested.

"Against a force as formidable as the god of destruction, we'd only get in his way," Alexa said.

"She's right. Michael would focus more on protecting us than on fighting against Lucifer," Julianna said.

"You're right," Ursula said with reluctance.

The girls nodded in agreement before taking formation. Alexa started the magic chant and the other girls joined. Almost instantly, their shadows rose into a shield, not even steel could perforate.

"I'll be the end to all your wildest dreams and so much more once this is over," Lucifer warned.

"What you call 'dreams', I call 'nightmares'. And I'll be the one to rid you from them, once and for all. I swear it," said Michael.

The hateful look on Michael's face suggested he could spit at the sight of this scoundrel, but Lucifer simply responded with a swaggering grin.

Enough of this! Michael thought to himself.

A chill rushed through his body as ancient power coursed through him. The skies responded with claps of lightning. A blanket of darkness shrouded the forest as creation and destruction set for battle.

CHAPTER 7
SECRETS FROM THE SHADOWS

Michael's eyes flared with disgust. Every fiber of his being seeped with hatred for the man facing off against him. His fingers inched towards the sword by his side. As they grazed the handle, he felt a jolt of self-doubt pierce his mind. It left him trembling, panting heavily as a cold sweat formed.

"Still afraid, I see." Lucifer grinned. "It's only natural when pitted against an opponent as formidable as me."

"What is it you want with me, Lucifer?" groaned Michael. "Do you just want our titan rings or are you trying to recreate one of your sick nightmares?"

"A true master of the dark arts never reveals his intentions until it's too late. Too late for his opponent, that is," Lucifer replied in a playful tone.

"I've had it with your mind games," Michael snapped. "Tell me what it is you want with me and those dimension titans or I swear I'll knock you out of this fucking dimension."

"You boast an impressive game for someone too timid to unsheathe his blade." Lucifer grinned.

Michael's face reddened. "We'll see who's timid!"

He couldn't hold back any longer. He swiped his blade out of its sheath and stormed forward with a trail of lightning.

Lucifer chuckled. He manifested an orb of shadows in his hand. The girls watched from the side with awe as it took the shape of a sword. Michael's blade edged closer before Lucifer struck him deep in the stomach.

Michael looked down at Lucifer's weapon, coughing up blood and gasping with disbelief. "That's"—

"Do you see now what it means to be the demon king?" said Lucifer. "I'm more than just a walker of dimensions and dreams. My ability to forge the very darkness to my whim is unparalleled."

"This feeling..." Michael twitched from the unbearable squirming inside him. "...it's like your shadows are swallowing me from the inside."

"Yes, shadows are the opposing element of the angel race. Being stricken by them is like having a flesh-eating disease dwell inside you."

"That can't be. Make it stop!" Michael grabbed onto the shadow blade, attempting to pull it out. Like a rabid hound thrice his size, it proved too strong. Fighting his will, it burrowed deeper, forcing out his screams.

"Michael!" Isabella shouted.

She and the others looked with terror as Michael's body gave out.

"God or liar or whatever, he's still our friend. We can't let him do this!" Ursula pleaded.

Lucifer smirked. "I'd avoid stepping closer. Unless you'd like to meet a similar fate. After all, history shows I'm not averse to slaughtering my own blood."

"You won't end me." Michael gritted his teeth, tearing up as blood spilled from his mouth. "I won't let you because my fate is mine to control."

"That might be true, but with fate comes resolve. And yours is too weak!" With his other fist, Lucifer thumped Michael square in the face, sending him off the shadows of his blade and to the ground.

Michael's eyes widened as he coughed up even more blood. He fell to his side, gasping in agony. The girls watched in horror. Ursula tried to intervene but Alexa blocked her, citing the immense danger of daring Lucifer.

"I'm getting bored, already. How about you and I give your little harem a performance to remember?"

Lucifer released his webbed black wings for the night to see. They expanded further than the girls' did. Michael leaned forward, more intimidated by Lucifer's power than before. Still, he refused to let his resolve go unrequited.

"Fine, if that's what you want, you've got it!" Michael stood up, releasing his white feathered wings.

Lucifer looked at him and grinned as Michael's wounds healed. "I see you're able to regenerate when you're in your angel form."

"That's right." Michael remembered his first booming of the archangel. Amidst the ruins of an elemental stricken city, the gashes left his stomach healed, and his ambitions born.

"Very nice. I'm glad this doesn't have to end so soon anymore. I was hoping to make a night out of this."

"In your dreams," Michael replied, lunging towards him with his sword.

"In that case, where in my dreams would you like to finish this?" Lucifer said, swiftly blocking Michael's attack.

"The one where I bury you!" Michael formed a pulsating stream of bolts in his hand and blasted Lucifer in the face, sending him a dozen feet back.

Lucifer hissed from the burning sensation as it took hold. His eyes grew red and veiny all around as they began to water.

"Shadows may be a flesh-eating disease to angels, but what

are lightning bolts to demons if not the equivalent?" Michael asked.

Lucifer stared with a flaring scowl. "You're more scrupulous than I thought."

"No kidding," Alexa said to the girls. "That was quick thinking on Michael's part."

"But how long can he maintain that momentum?" Julianna asked.

Lucifer and Michael rushed at each other with their blades. Their blades clashed, forcing a storm of lightning and shadow across the battlefield. The girls screamed as they shielded themselves from the blow.

As the dome-like explosion of black and white slowly dissipated, it revealed the ongoing ferocious combat. Michael and Lucifer exchanged swings of their swords and various light and dark based attacks, respectively.

"You're not half bad for someone with hardly any recollection of who they are," Lucifer said.

"It doesn't take a powerful memory to know you can't be trusted," Michael refuted.

The two continued to clash their blades, trading blows and splattering blood upon the battlefield.

"Damn, this is hard to watch!" Ursula said in a nervous state, as she covered her eyes with her hand, peeking through her fingers.

"Michael will do fine. He just needs to believe in himself," Julianna said in a more calm and collected manner.

"Therein lies the problem," said Alexa.

"What do you mean?" Ursula asked.

"I mean Michael talks a big game, but I doubt he has what it takes to carry out the victory he needs."

"Yeah, but"—Ursula began.

"Let's not forget his powers have been dormant for years

and his memory is still fledgling. Meanwhile, Lucifer's power is at full capacity."

"What are you saying?" Isabella asked.

Alexa sighed. "I'm saying Michael can believe in his ambitions all he wants, but his power just won't be able to match Lucifer's in the end."

"I think you're wrong," Ursula said.

"Just look at his battling tactics of you don't believe me," Alexa said. "He's very good at sending out his lightning attacks and he's decent with his sword, but he'll need to do more to win this. The last thing he wants is to focus on what he desires out of his future, he blinds himself from what's in front of him."

"You're right," Julianna said. "We're dealing with a ruthless tyrant that toys with his victims and won't stop until he gets what he wants."

What does he want? Our rings? Or is he here for something more? Ursula thought as a feeling of fright surged in her.

Lucifer swung his blade and struck Michael cleanly. Michael tumbled to the ground with blood gushing out of his mouth.

It only infuriated him more. He slowly returned to his feet and said, "That's it. I've had it with you."

Lucifer laughed. "Do you really think you're fooling anyone? We both know you're only a fraction of the being you once were. Why don't you give up this little battle and hand your titan rings over?"

"Not to a man who seeks to use them for evil," said Michael.

"Really? And what's so evil about wanting to gather all the titans together to protect the dimensions again?" Lucifer asked.

"Protect them? Bullshit! All you're capable of is destroying each way you turn," said Michael.

"I'm hurt you'd think so little of me," Lucifer replied in a playful tone. "I simply want to give our little omniverse the care that it needs to thrive."

"I've seen the way you treat the people around you." Michael grimaced at the memory of the bruises Hecate had during their previous encounter among the elementals. The shades of blue she wore still left him shaking with resentment. "A man like you isn't capable of protecting anything or anyone."

Lucifer looked back with a nefarious grin curling wider across his face. "Allow me to make things very simple, then. Without the unification of the titans, the dimensions have gone out of control."

"What are you talking about?" Michael said in a flustered tone.

"Look around at the world you live in. A lot of unjust behavior taking place, right? Political and legal malpractice and unethical business tactics. Even the officials are tainted by the stain that is human depravity," said Lucifer.

"Human depravity? What are you getting at?" Michael wondered.

"Humanity is the source of all the world's problems, Michael. Believe me. The other six dimensions have it just as bad. As soon as a single human enters a dimension, village, or region, for that matter, they instantly plague it with their false promises of prosperity and moral ambiguity."

Michael remembered his experiences in the various cities of both realms clearly. He witnessed much of their unbridled cruelty for himself, be it from the officials, the townspeople, or his former masters.

"They're a detriment to everyone and everything around them. Countless races over the eons have fallen to their ways. When I capture all seven titans, the first thing I will do is destroy humankind. Then, I will revive all other races they've slaughtered over the years, restoring this omniverse to the way it once was."

"Wait, you'd bring them back?"

Michael's eyes widened with wonder as Lucifer's nightmarish words turned to almost a dream. Michael saw a world where those the humans condemned as unworthy could thrive again. The prospect filled him with envy.

"That's correct," Lucifer said. "However, I can't do that last part on my own. That's where you come in."

"Excuse me?" Michael said, confused, as he wiped the blood from his mouth.

"You see, a destroyer god can only destroy. To revive, I must create. Join me, Michael. Together, we can restore this omniverse to the way it once was," said Lucifer.

"The way it once was?" Michael wondered, puzzled by the notion of things ever having been so different. He found the idea enticing. Shortly, his feet shuffled towards Lucifer without his control.

"Michael, don't listen to him!" Alexa shouted.

"Silence!" With a ferocious swing of his arm, Lucifer cast forth a wall of shadow from the ground, knocking the four of them over.

"Don't listen to those fools, Michael..." Lucifer began, "... we can make things as they were before the age of humanity, but even better. There will be no war, no conflict, or corruption. Races of all types will live in harmony, worshipping their gods and the titans. Together, we can create this utopia. As the two king pieces that rule over the board of existence. What do you say?" Lucifer reached out his hand.

"Easy to have no wars when everyone's already been slaughtered," Julianna said to herself.

Michael looked at the sinisterly grinning Lucifer. He couldn't decide on what to say. The only thought on his mind was the pain he experienced growing up.

"No government corruption and no money to poison the minds of the powerful? All those things you said, they'll all go away when the humans die off?" Michael wondered, inching out his hand.

"Indeed," Lucifer said, smiling.

"Don't do it, he's lying to you!" said Isabella.

"Enough from the lot of you, already," Lucifer demanded. "The men are busy at work."

"Well, the women would like a say, as well. And we say you can't be trusted," Isabella announced, matter-of-factly.

"These are just delusions of grandeur you're feeding him. Regardless of how he may have deceived us, I won't allow it," Julianna shouted.

"Julianna. All of you."

Michael turned towards the girls. The welcoming smiles on their faces told him he had gained back a piece of their trust. He responded with a smile.

"I'd watch your tone if I were you. I can end you with a snap of my fingers," said Lucifer.

Lucifer looked back at Michael. "Just shake my hand and we can rule over this omniverse together. It's that simple," said Lucifer.

"Rule it?" said Michael.

"Yes, you and I will have absolute power over this world. No one will defy the gods of creation and destruction," he assured.

Michael went into careful thought. *His power is unlike anything I've ever experienced. That much is clear from our battle, and I'm sure he's holding back a tremendous amount.*

He watched in pensive silence as Lucifer's devious grin grew with every passing moment. Thoughts raced across his mind.

Lucifer was more powerful than the girls, no question about that. In fact, he was leagues beyond them.

The pressure of the dilemma built, then Michael made his decision.

"You're refusing?" said Lucifer in shock. The girls all sighed with smiles of relief.

Michael grinned. "I'll admit; I was tempted at first. After all, these damn humans have been the bane of my existence these last twenty years. But when you said you're in it for the power and not just to fix this world, that's when I knew."

"Knew what?" Lucifer asked.

"That you were nothing more than a dirty lying snake!"

Michael stomped forward, hurling a punch towards Lucifer's face. Lucifer caught it with ease.

"I suggest you reconsider. There's far more to having power than simply abusing it."

"That's what you think," said Michael.

"That's what I know. With the two of us, we can"—

"We can what?" Michael cut him off. "We can return these former races, just to enslave them? Tell me, how would that make us better than the humans?"

"I never suggested such a thing. I desire to give the races free will. Yes, we'd rule over them as dual overlords, but we would force no ideals over them. The world is essentially theirs for the taking."

"Sounds too good to be true. A lot like those false promises of prosperity and moral ambiguity you mentioned before!" said Michael.

"Humanity's left you bitter and untrusting, hasn't it, Michael?" Lucifer asked. "Keeping secrets all to yourself."

"Enough trying to turn me to your maniacal ways!"

"Just what are you telling me; that the world is better off with humans? Surely not," said Lucifer.

"That's not what I'm saying at all. Fuck humans."

"Then, why not"—

"You can talk about free will all you want, but at the end of the day, it's guided by power. And power is an aggravator of evil. Something that has only taken a temporary haven in the humans, it'll find a new haven elsewhere soon enough," said Michael.

"Excuse me?!" Lucifer said, taken aback.

"If not the humans, then some other race will plague this world," Michael said, aiming a punch to Lucifer's stomach.

Lucifer caught this punch, as well, with his other hand. He twisted Michael's fist towards the ground, stopping him in place as he scowled with malice from his defiant words.

Lucifer replied, "That is ridiculous! You've lived so long among the humans, you've forgotten the true nature of power. Under the right command, we can save this world from itself. Don't you understand?"

"Especially when it's you who rules with me."

"Things like evil and power are not exclusive to humans." Michael gritted his teeth. "And I don't care about ruling omniverse. I just want a peaceful life with my friends. If I can become rich, too, even better."

"And your allies say I preach delusion." Lucifer smirked.

"Besides, if we destroy the humans, we'll just end up going for the next race to cross us. My friends are right. We'll wipe out one after that until there's nothing left. Is that what you want? To rule over an empty kingdom on the mountain of your slain subordinates?" Michael shouted emphatically.

"Michael..." Isabella said, lost for words.

"I'm incredibly cynical and distrustful. That's just how I am. While I try to see the good in everything, I can also see the bad. Yes, humans are terrible, but their terrible nature could be hiding the less negative qualities of other races just waiting for the opportunity to flourish in the wake of humanity's demise. And as bad as humans are, another race could be even worse. You'd have only yourself to blame for enabling them once the humans are gone! We'd be digging this world into its own grave, don't you see?"

The girls looked at him and smiled.

"He's certainly wiser than he leads on," Alexa said, wide-eyed.

"His past as a god becomes more convincing with every word he says," Ursula added.

Lucifer grinned. "Well, as the creator god, you'll have to make some sacrifices. Even if it means wiping the slate clean and starting anew."

Michael sneered. "I figured you'd say something like that. And I don't care. You want to know why?"

"Humor me," said Lucifer.

"I have a life of my own. That's what I'm fighting for. I don't care what you do with the titans, the dimensions, or the humans. Let them fight until their death, for all I fucking care. I just want to be left alone to live as I please. To hell with this power or all that shit. I just want peace."

"I see now." Lucifer grinned. "So, it's not that you want to stop my endeavors. You just don't want to get involved. Spoken like a negligent parent."

Michael met him with an icy stare. "Look at it however you want. I may be a god, but I have no interest in acting like one. Good or bad, I just want to live as I please."

"How selfish," Lucifer said with a sneer. "Tell me, is that lifestyle worth it to you or are you just accustomed to living a life of mediocrity and don't feel like achieving something greater?"

"Quiet!" Michael roared. "I'll live my life how I want. So, stop acting as if you have me figured out when you don't!"

"Oh, you and I both know that's not true. I know you grew up in the Asmodai household and that you were abused until the end of your days there. I know you drown your sorrows in beer and hard liquor. You may have recently quit, but we both know it won't last long. Also, I know you're a total lecher," said Lucifer.

"What?" Michael exclaimed.

"Don't tell me you don't lust after your friends. I know you can't resist having lewd, perverted, and depraved thoughts about the girls you call your friends. How pathetic. You turn down their advances, just to fantasize about them later. Wake up, you fool! The opportunity is right in front of you. It always has been. The women. Power. The peaceful lifestyle as a ruler of a world without conflict. Stop making excuses for yourself and make the world your own! Nothing comes easy, and if you really want what you say you want, you must fight for it!" said Lucifer.

Michael smiled. "You're right."

"Wait, he is?" Isabella asked.

"Not about much, but he is right that things in life never come easy," Michael replied. His body began to glow a bright white. "Even a peaceful life is never devoid of conflict. With that sentiment in mind, take this! Lightwave of retribution!"

A burst of claymores encased in lightning hurtled from the misty clouds above. Everyone watched them descend, in awe.

"Finally, an actual attack. Well, I guess I should try, as well." Lucifer pointed his blade towards the ground.

"Go Darkwave of annihilation!"

From the soil came a barrage of darkened daggers from the shadows. The two waves of blades crashed into each other, destroying everything on impact as everyone fought to retain their balance from the rippling impact.

"It seems like our attacks were evenly matched," Michael said, peering over his arm.

Lucifer smirked. From the ground came the eruption of his next assault. No swords. Rather, a slew of narrow inky hands.

They latched towards Michael's ankles, seeking to drag him down. He refused to let such a fate befall him. With a swing of his scepter, he unleashed a slew of bright discs with serrated edges. Like saws, they sliced through the field of hands reaching towards him. Their ink splattered across the grass.

The girls watched from the sidelines, stunned as Michael maneuvered his way through Lucifer's defense until his scepter reached a fist's distance towards his opponent's face. The demon king struck back with his swords once again. Together, they found themselves back at one another's necks.

Sweat rolled down their faces. A different sword blocked each of Michael's swings. Beads of sweat rolled down Lucifer's neck as he grinned with elation.

"Yes, it appears our brief discussion has strengthened you. As you grow in power, your memories return. Tell me. What do you remember from your days as the creator god?" Lucifer said with a smile.

Michael stared at him blankly. "Honestly, nothing. I still can't remember much else about my time before this life."

"Well, it sounds to me like you need a little more motivation," Lucifer said, lunging his blade towards Michael. Michael blocked the sword with his own.

Michael and Lucifer thrust their way into the sky, sending a burst of dust flying. The battle raged, getting mightier and more destructive. They matched each other, blow for blow, spell for spell, and blood for blood.

"Motivate me all you want. It'll be your undoing, as it only makes me stronger," said Michael.

Lucifer grinned. "We'll see how strong you are without your sword!"

With a violent swing of his shadow blade, Lucifer made a clean incision through Michael's blade. Michael watched in disbelief as the fragment tumbled to the ground.

"My sword. No," he said with dread.

"Did you honestly think a cheap piece of iron could withstand the will of my shadows?" Lucifer asked.

Michael trembled with terror as he stared at the remains of his sword. Gritting his teeth, he shattered the remnants with his lightning.

"Not at all. Fortunately, that wasn't the only weapon in my possession."

He manifested a golden scepter in his hand. Its glow was so blinding, Lucifer shielded his eyes for a moment before they could readjust.

Lucifer smiled. "Very impressive, indeed. Don't forget, I still have plenty of tricks up my sleeve. You have a long way to go before you can defeat me."

"What, are you going to dispatch another one of your minions on me?" Michael said, sending a lightning burst enchantment at Lucifer's face.

Lucifer flew around it and looked at him with a sly grin. "Oh, Hecate? She was the worst combination of weak and arrogant, wasn't she?"

He sent out a dark beam attack at Michael, hitting him successfully in the face, nearly knocking him out of the sky.

"How could you say that? She loved you! She may have been psychotic, but she gave her life away for you!" Michael shouted, pushing harder.

"A pawn may fall here and there, but never lose sight of the king," Lucifer said, pushing back.

Michael gritted his teeth, both from the pressure of the dark magic beam pressing him towards the ground and the callous words from the one who cast it.

"You fucking hypocrite!" he shouted, sending light beams towards Lucifer.

"I didn't say pawns were useless. Quite the contrary, I never would have found you all so easily if not for you capturing her titan ring. Furthermore, only weak mortals would use such weak constructs as hypocrisy to define a man. Call me what you will, but I'm the destroyer god, first and foremost," Lucifer said, pushing Michael with his blade.

Michael looked straight into Lucifer's eyes as he pushed back with his sword. "Whatever accolades you think you have with that title, I'll match them and raise you the largest ass-kicking you've ever gotten."

He blasted Lucifer in the face and watched him fall from the sky. Lucifer landed with a thundering thud that sent bursts of energy flying. The shadows writhed with his collapse.

Michael flew down to the ground and walked towards Lucifer's unconscious body. The girls removed their barricade and ran towards Michael with shock and excitement.

"You did it! That was amazing!" Ursula said, hugging him, tightly.

"You defeated the demon king!" Isabella shouted just as jovially.

"I wouldn't be so sure," Michael said, looking over at Lucifer's body.

"What do you mean? He's out cold," said Isabella.

"I doubt it. The destroyer won't go down with one attack," said Julianna.

"She's right. Let's take a look," said Alexa.

They cautiously approached Lucifer. He then struggled back up with a groan. They watched intensely as his crow mask cracked, revealing his face. As the pieces fell, Michael and the girls looked at him in stunned silence.

"No way. This must be some mistake!" Michael said, "Why does he"—

Lucifer brushed the black hair away from his crimson eyes. "Oh, this is no mistake, Michael. The face you see is your own. Because I am you."

Michael froze in shock with no logical words to come out of his mouth as he stared into a mirror image of his face.

CHAPTER 8
STAR CROSSED RIVALS

"Tell me this is some sort of spell," Michael said, still in disbelief.

"I'm afraid not, for not even the strongest demon could perform an enchantment powerful enough to replicate what you see before you now. What you see is the truth," Lucifer said, smiling.

"And what is the truth? That you're some sort of copy of me?" Michael asked.

Lucifer looked at him, pondering over the question. "I think it would be best to say you and I are twin brothers. Born from the same chaos that was this omniverse before it became what you see today."

"You and I are brothers?" Michael said. He didn't think he could get any more stunned.

"Indeed, we are," said Lucifer.

The girls watched their exchange, utterly mesmerized.

"Just when I thought this couldn't get more absurd, Lucifer tells us he's brothers with Michael? Ridiculous!" said Isabella.

"This doesn't surprise me," Alexa said, calmly.

"What? Are you saying he's telling the truth?" Isabella asked.

"I'm saying there are some legends from my home dimension, albeit rather scarce, that depict these gods as having a special bond, not unlike that of a family. I don't think this is some sort of coincidence or act of magic. No, I think they are, as he said, twin brothers born from the same chaos," said Alexa.

"No way!" said Isabella in disbelief. "I've known him all my life as just my brother. Now, he's so much I never knew him to be. The archangel, a god, and the brother of this sadistic asshole. Who is our friend, really?"

"It's alright." Julianna patted her on the shoulder. "He's still our friend."

"What I want to know is how twin brothers came to be so different? Our Michael is so sweet and Lucifer's so gross," said Ursula.

"Whatever happened, that face definitely goes better with blue eyes and white hair," said Alexa. The other girls nodded in agreement.

Meanwhile, Lucifer looked at Michael with a devious grin. "So, would you like to pick up where we left off?"

"I thought you'd never ask," Michael said, raising his scepter.

"Good, because I think it's time I stop holding back." From his shadows, Lucifer forged a scepter identical to his. Michael's eyes widened.

"Surprised to see I carry the same weapon?"

Michael sneered. "Not in the slightest."

"Very good. That means you're getting it now."

Lucifer surprised Michael with a swing of his scepter, slicing his neck open with the end. Michael vomited blood as blood gushed through his fingers covering the wound.

"How did you?" Michael said, dropping to his knees.

"That's the power of a destroyer god. My speed is otherworldly. I wouldn't expect a weak little god with amnesia to understand that," Lucifer said before repeatedly stabbing Michael in the chest and stomach with the end of his scepter.

Michael could no longer hold back his screams, as the pain became unbearable. "It's a good thing you're immortal. Otherwise, my fun would have ended a long time ago." Kicking Michael while he was down. "Unfortunately, that means there's no end to the level of pain you can experience. And every ounce, you'll fucking feel!"

"Stop it! You're hurting him." Against her fear, Ursula rushed towards Michael, ready to help.

"Don't worry about me," Michael whimpered as he attempted to stand up straight. "I can handle him on my own."

"I don't care," Ursula refuted. "This battle needs to end before"—

"Before what? You'll take his spot?" Lucifer asked.

Ursula looked at him, unsure of what to say before stepping back.

"That's what I thought. Your lives are only temporary, whereas Michael's suffering can forever endure. Would you give up your life to keep Michael from taking any more damage, assuming I was even that generous?" Lucifer inquired with a smirk.

"That's enough!" Alexa shouted. "Don't pick on her!"

"After all, what's stopping me from killing you all, dead, or making you my servants? I'm clearly the superior one here, and your pathetic friend knows it. He should concede," Lucifer exclaimed.

Tears rolled down Ursula's face.

"It's alright, Ursula. Michael will pull through," said Isabella, holding her in a comforting embrace.

"I hate feeling so helpless. He's in so much pain and we can't do anything," Ursula whimpered.

"That's not true," said Alexa.

"What?" Ursula wondered.

"Alexa's right. We can still believe in him. Remember. They're gods, so they are immortal. In other words, this battle only ends when someone yields. As long as Michael can push forward, he'll rise above that prick of a twin brother," said Julianna.

"But, what if he can't?" Ursula suggested. The eyes of the other three sharply turned towards her with worry.

"What if he hurts himself so bad, falls into a comatose state?" Ursula asked.

"Ursula..." Alexa began with a lachrymose stare. "...I don't think he"—

"We know he lost his memories when he entered a long sleep, but we don't know how the sleep began," Ursula continued.

"It was because"—

"Because a winner couldn't be decided," Alexa said with a fearful gaze before Julianna could finish her sentence. The words Lucifer said about the battle he and Michael had long ago were even more haunting now.

"Are you suggesting"—Isabella's eyes widened.

"If Michael pushes himself, he'll lose all the memories he's gained back. And we'll lose the person we've come to know."

Despair dropped like boulders down to the bottoms of their chests as they watched the battle continue. They shared in the hope of the battle coming to a swift end.

The four of them looked at each other, nodding. Michael fell on his back, full of punctures from the scepter. Lucifer looked down and grinned.

"It seems our battle is over. Oh, well. If you can't get up, I'll take this little nap of yours as your resignation."

Michael looked up into Lucifer's eyes, and then slowly closed his. His mind mildly slipped out of consciousness.

"Don't you dare give up!" Julianna shouted.

"Julianna?" Michael said, inching his head towards her.

"Listen. If you don't win this, I don't know how long any of us will be around," said Julianna.

"Couldn't we at least use the titans to protect ourselves?" Ursula whispered.

"And draw ourselves onto the battlefield? Again, not a good idea," Alexa replied.

Titan rings, Lucifer thought with a devious grin. *I almost forgot.*

"You were right before. The man is a brute. The proof, alone, is in the way he treated Hecate. He can't be trusted," said Isabella.

"Don't forget, Michael. We still believe in you, no matter what," said Ursula.

"Yes. If anyone can knock him out, it's you," Alexa added.

Michael smiled as his wounds began to heal. "Thank you," he said under his breath.

Lucifer looked at him in amusement. "So, you rely on the encouragement of your friends for strength. I see that weakness now."

"What weakness is there in having friends who believe in me?" Michael said as he rose to his feet.

"Simple. You have to rely on them to get the edge you need," said Lucifer. "And fall when they aren't around."

"And how is that a sign of being weak?" Michael refuted with faint pant.

Lucifer laughed. "How is it not? A demon never relies on anyone else to win a battle. Wasting your time depending on others will get you killed."

"Well, I'm no demon, so I play by my own fucking rules!" Michael exclaimed, striking Lucifer with his scepter.

Lucifer knocked Michael's scepter out of his hand with his own. "I told you I was no longer holding back, right? Now, it's time to put those words into action."

A familiar chill filled the air. The same he felt when he arrived in Lucifer's castle: the wretched miasma that filled the halls.

"I know that feeling. What are you up to?" Michael said, panicking.

The girls screamed when a horrific sensation overtook them. Fear coursed through Michael as he watched a slew of inky streams permeate from their chests. It was as if they had their souls drained.

"Lucifer, stop this now!"

"I'd rather not, but thanks for the suggestion!"

The girls grew weaker from the plaque-induced air around them. The air felt thinner as their bodies grew frail. They could hardly stand or fight back the unrelenting agony brought upon by the demon king's surge of wrath.

"What have you done to them?" Michael shouted as he watched them all drop to their hands and knees.

"Oh, not much. I've simply taken a couple of things from them," said Lucifer.

The girls had now grown so weak they collapsed across the ground.

"You monster! Stop this now," Michael demanded.

"Oh, don't worry about them. This is only a minor side effect of my plunder magic," said Lucifer.

"Plunder?"

"Yes, my plunder magic allows me to steal anything I want. Spells, a fledgling thought, or even just an item. And of course, someone's dreams," said Lucifer.

"That's fucking insane! Is that how you enter my dreams so easily?" Michael asked.

"Partially. That's a part of my *dreamwalking* magic. It

allows me to enter and alter them as I please. Enough of that, though. Aren't you curious to know what I took from them?" Lucifer asked.

"It crossed my mind," Michael replied bitterly.

"Good, then you should be able to recognize what I have in store for you. Especially since you've fought them before!" Lucifer raised his scepter high. As two rings appeared on his fingers.

"No way! Are those?"—

"That's right," Lucifer replied. "They're the titans you defeated during your last two battles. And here they are again."

"This can't be!"

The skies raged in chaos, sifting and swirling into a vortex to prepare for the arrival of two ancient denizens from outer worlds.

"Come forth! Tiamat, titan of the first dimension; and Lycanthrope, titan of the second dimension!"

With his command, the skies tore open to make way for the monolithic vulture. Its shadow cast darkness upon them as it flew past the bloody moon, spirally downwards to land. Its deafening squawk echoed chillingly through the silence. Meanwhile, a rattle on the ground turned into a violent rumble. Cracks emerged before it gave way, splitting open to let out the werewolf.

Michael stared, horrified by the creatures as they both roared into the weeping skies.

"Unreal. You summoned two titans at once?"

"That's the difference in power between a mere demon and the king of all demons," Lucifer smugly said as he looked over at the girls.

"Summon whatever you want. I've beaten them before and I'll beat them again!" said Michael.

He beat his wings against the shadow and gripped his scepter tightly before flying towards the titans. He soared until he was at eye level with the beasts.

"That may be true, but I can assure you facing two titans at once will make for a very different experience," Lucifer warned.

"We'll just see about that!" Michael said, pointing his scepter towards them.

Lucifer smiled confidently. "Yes, we will."

"Great scepter, wipe Tiamat out with blinding lightwave of retribution!" Michael commanded. A colossal wave of claymores rained from the sky. They broke through the starry night, rushing in the bird's direction.

"You're using that weak enchantment again?" Lucifer sifted through the shadows and reappeared into the night, hovering just a dozen feet from where Michael was.

"It's far different," Michael said.

"Oh?"

"The light these swords emit is far greater," Michael explained. "No dark based magic can resist or escape its touch. What's more is that they won't stop until they hit their target. In other words, your oversized bird can fly to each end of the omniverse and my claymores will be there waiting."

"What an intriguing theory." Lucifer chuckled.

"Huh?"

Just as the claymores were about to hit Tiamat, Lycanthrope howled at the moon and deflected the attack effortlessly. Each blade fazed into his fur. Like rays swallowed by the darkness, they were no more.

"What? That wolf blocked all my swords," Michael said.

"How right you are, my friend. Are you seeing the direness in your situation now? Your claymores may pursue an enemy until the end of time, but if the howls of my beast wash your attack out, then I'm afraid it nullifies your attack. That's the price when you try focusing your energy on one beast at a time when you should have been focusing on them both!" said Lucifer.

Focus on them both? Michael thought. *Perhaps he has a point.*

"I hope your next assault won't be so pathetic in execution. Titans all have an innate ability that allows them to protect one another in the heat of battle without fail. What's more is Tiamat can conceal the magical characteristics of an attack, so the blades you cast are already weakened upon arrival. It makes them easier for Lycanthrope to absorb," said Lucifer.

"So, they protected each other? Ironic someone who doesn't believe in teamwork would know so much about it," said Michael.

"It takes a well-educated man to know what's right and what's wrong. I may not believe in teamwork, but I believe in having servants. And that's what these titans are to me. Not guardians. Not friends. They're servants. Pawns for my bidding."

"Again with your pawns and your servants? And you wonder why I don't want to rule with you as dual kings," said Michael.

"Say what you want about my methods, but my pawns are doing an excellent job of taking you down. Even a master such as myself needs his servants. Why do you think I'm collecting the titans for in the first place?"

Collecting? You stole those titans from my friends, he thought to himself, looking over at them.

A smug smile formed on Michael's face. "Sounds like you can't take over the omniverse without them."

"I can't do it without you, either, so forfeit and this world will be ours!" said Lucifer.

"Never!"

"Then, I'll force your will to become my own!" Lucifer shouted as Tiamat struck Michael with his claw, knocking him out of the sky and onto the ground.

Lucifer looked down at Michael. He was like an ant, both from the distance and the way he was spited with no resistance.

"How sad. You preach the importance of friendship and having moral character. Yet, you fall like such a fucking embarrassment. Ridiculous. The humans of this world must have plagued your mind. Perhaps a little motivation from my dreamwalking magic will help," Lucifer said, chuckling under his breath.

Michael laid there, tossing and turning as if having a terrible nightmare. Deep in his subconscious was exactly that. The same darkness he felt time and time again, tugging at his body without end or remorse.

❀❀❀

"WHERE AM I?"

Michael found himself walking through an abandoned village. It was unlike any village he'd seen before. It was as if it came from another time. A time long before his.

Michael walked through an abandoned village, not unlike the one he grew up in back in the Dark Realm. The buildings were modest and crafted with dark shades of wood and stone, with bazaars lined across either side of the street. It all seemed rather ordinary—dull, even. Yet, there was a growing emptiness beyond the lack of people. Like a black hole pulling him in deeper.

Something isn't right. This village seems to come a time long before mine. How can that be?

He ventured through the village streets. The vacant alleyways and unattended merchant stands left his legs trembling with fear.

This place feels so familiar, and yet I've seen nothing like this.

Michael noticed a stranger carrying her groceries. Many small children quickly followed.

Michael ran towards them with his arm out. "Excuse me, ma'am. What town are we in?" The woman did not respond or even acknowledge his presence. As if nothing more than phantoms, they all walked straight through him, unimpeded.

"How is that even possible?" Michael said, confused as he frantically turned around. He saw the bazaars were filled with other people. He wondered if they would walk through him just the same. Afraid to find out, sweat beaded down his face.

He broke into a panicked run, looking over his shoulder and into diverging streets for anyone to provide some information. He turned to a nearby market and navigated through the stands to a man selling chickens.

"Sir, excuse me. I need help!" As he reached out his hand, it went right through the table.

"It's true. It's as if I don't exist. But, why?" Michael wondered.

The search for answers led him out of the town's borders and to the outskirts, where he found a massive estate with grand and demonic ornamentation. He climbed up the gate and jumped to the other side with a heavy pant.

"Why does this place feel so familiar too? Even more so than the village," Michael said as he ran through the door.

As he reached out for the circular stone handle, he stopped himself, realizing it was no use.

"Right, if I don't exist, I most likely won't be able to open this door. Perhaps, I can just walk through it?" he said to himself.

Michael took a deep breath and closed his eyes before

taking a step forward. He continued to walk when he opened his eyes, finding himself on the other side of the door.

He looked around and saw two spiral staircases, one on either side of the room. The walls were adorned with tapestry, all obscured by shadows. With a nervous gulped, he proceeded up the creaking steps of the righthand side staircase before making his way down the corridors where the shadows awaited.

"This place is spectacular!" he said, as he gazed upon all the goat statues and horns all across the walls and ceilings.

"I wonder what sort of people live here."

Michael heard a noise in this seemingly vacant room. He dashed further down the hall to see what made the noise.

He stood in a room of black shadowy figures with a familiar aura. There were about a dozen of them ranging from one large, a medium, and several tiny ones.

"Big family of shadows, I guess."

The shadowy figures were still. Michael stepped on a loose floorboard and drew the attention of the shadows. They moved towards him.

"Oh, no! They can see me?" Michael said to himself.

The eerie sounds of the faceless beings frightened Michael. They communicated in a tongue akin to ceaseless murmurs Michael couldn't understand. He ran as far from them as he could, panting with dread when he noticed them looming over his shoulders. He crashed through the floor, falling for a period that felt eternal and screaming out before noticing something strange. Something out of place in any reality.

I was only on the second floor, but I've been falling for what feels like an eternity. And those shadows looking up at me don't seem to get any smaller, Michael thought as he gazed at the blank expressions on their faces. Though he couldn't see any eyes or mouths to speak of, he sensed they were curious.

"Is this what my life's come down to; falling out of control with nothing but these faceless things watching me fall to a death that will never happen? The epitome of futility, it seems. What a nightmare I've been dealt."

Suddenly, he had an epiphany. "Wait a minute. A nightmare? Am I dreaming?"

He looked all around, sensing the dark energy of nightmares prior.

"I am, aren't I? This reality makes little sense. I'm sure Lucifer has something to do with this, just like he always has. But what? Why can't I remember? It's like all I can focus on is this estate."

He took a deep breath, staring at the family of darkened figments hanging over him.

"Perhaps, these are images from my past. That's why it all feels so familiar, despite my lack of memory of this place. I see that now. The village, the estate, and those shadows. It's all a part of a bigger picture, isn't it?"

Michael nodded and clenched his fists. In his mind, he honed in on his many years of abuse and the friendships that followed, determined to hold on to them, no matter the opposition he faced.

"I don't know what that picture will look like in the end, but I know every fragment is critical to its foundation. So, I'm not about to lie here, suspended in midair forever, wondering what it will be in the end. No. It's time to wake up because, now, I know who I am, who I am not, and who I'm destined to become!"

❧

MICHAEL WOKE UP TO THE SOUND OF THE TITANS ROARING on the battlefield. He smiled as he rose to his feet.

"I was correct. That was nothing more than a dream."

Lucifer grinned. "Sweet ones, were they? Did you see anything interesting?"

"Indeed, I did. Believe me; you'll be sorry you ever put that enchantment on me," Michael replied, flying back up to where he was, across Lucifer.

"Really, and why is that?" Lucifer asked.

"Because now you've given me a whole new reason to defeat you," said Michael.

"Is that so?"

"Yes, I'll admit my goals were selfish. I wanted a life of luxury, despite having no ambitions of making my own money. I wanted to keep my friends, even though I showed no effort in becoming strong enough to protect them."

He thought of the many mornings he'd slept in under the influence of liquor, wondering how much time he would have allowed himself to waste. How long any of what he had would stay before leaving him behind.

"And I also hated humans but refused to put any effort into dealing with them myself. What's worse is I thought you were right when you said I could never amount to anything beyond mediocrity. But now"—

"Now, what? You've changed just like that?" Lucifer wondered. "What exactly did you see?"

"Are you saying you don't know?" Michael grinned. "I take it then you have no control over my dreams if you're not there to see them?"

"Well played. You've found the weakness in my magic," said Lucifer.

"That's right. And I just saw a glimpse of my past," said Michael.

"Really?" Lucifer raised an eyebrow.

"Yes. I don't know what any of it means, but it's my life and I could feel its overwhelming significance and the warm embrace it brought to my heart. If defeating you is what it takes to uncover my past and learn of what it all meant, then defeating you is what I'll do," said Michael.

"And you really feel that defeating me will help you accomplish this?"

"I know fighting you this far has brought me closer. So perhaps by defeating you, I'll know who I am and what my ultimate purpose was. In fact, I think it's my destiny to do just that."

"Destiny? What a joke!" Lucifer scoffed.

"Say what you want, but I doubt you'll be able to handle what I have in store for you," Michael said as his aura grew.

"What's that supposed to mean?"

The increasing strength of Michael's glow illuminated his face. Fear and confusion replaced the smugness on Lucifer's as the angelic aura around Michael became so bright it consumed the shadows of the night.

"It's simple, Lucifer. You see, you're not the only one with the capacity to take a battle to the next level," Michael replied with a grin.

As if pushing with all the force his body could muster, Michael screamed from the depth of his lungs, harnessing the power inside and around him. Bolts of lightning struck the ground. Lucifer watched—mesmerized by the cracking ground. The forests quickly caught fire from the violent bursts of lightning.

"It seems I was a bit too generous with my dreamwalking magic. It's allowed you not only to regain a fragment of who you were, but also the power you possessed.

Lucifer sighed before grinning. "Oh, well. That just means I'm ahead of schedule. Not a problem."

Michael's eyes glowed even brighter and his hair grew longer, falling below his shoulders. He then unfurled two more sets of wings from his back, just before a burst of light blinded the battlefield.

"The light. It fucking burns!" Lucifer grunted, covering his eyes

Feeling the darkness return, Lucifer caught his breath and opened his eyes to a Michael of a different caliber.

"An etherial angel." Lucifer smiled. "It's about time."

"Time, indeed," Michael replied. "Now, it's time to end this battle. But before I do, there's one more creature that must be called to the battlefield."

"What did you just say?"

Lucifer gasped, watching in utter shock as a purple ring appeared around Michael's finger.

"You have a titan ring?" Lucifer's shock quickly turned into a grin. "Now, there's something I didn't see coming. Too bad you can't use it."

"That's what you think!" said Michael, raising his scepter.

Lucifer's face succumbed to a flustered expression as he watched the skies quake with the presence of the guardian behind the ring.

No, he thought. *He can't.*

"Mighty slayer of dwarves and ruler of orcs, I beseech you. Grace this veracious battle with your unwavering strength, so that together we may emerge victorious. Come forth! Obelisk, titan of the third dimension!"

A towering beast broke from the earth. A mountain of bulky muscle in gray metallic skin, with no head on its neck; simply a stream of teeth surrounding its circular jaws like a vortex, where its head would have been.

"I know this beast. This is the orc king that singlehand-edly defeated the dwarfish army but lost its head as a result? But how did you come across such a beast and how you can summon it?"

Lucifer gulped. His breath heightened as the titan's shadow loomed over him.

"I am the creator god, Lucifer. There's nothing I can't do!

That also goes for all those that stand beside me. Including my titan. Now, Obelisk! Show Lucifer and his legion what it truly means to be king!"

"What it means to be-"

Before Lucifer could finish his thought, there was shaking upon the land. So violently, he nearly fell over. The headless orc stormed forward and hurled his fist at Lycanthrope's face. The werewolf's eyes glowed a bright red like Lucifer's.

"Lycanthrope, counter with Transylvanian howling right now!" He demanded.

The werewolf nodded before unhinging its jaws. With its paws clenched, it was ready to silence its opposition.

Michael smirked. "It seems it's your memory failing you this time."

Lucifer's eyes widened. A realization even he'd forgotten at that moment sank in as he gazed at the menacing aura permeating from the headless orc.

"There's a hierarchy among the titans," Michael began. "The higher the number dimension from which it derives, the stronger it is."

"How well you recall." Lucifer sneered.

"In other words, the titan of the third dimension has absolute superiority over the titans of the first and second dimension," Michael said.

"So it does," Lucifer replied. "Strong pieces, as I'm sure you also remember, aren't enough to win the battle. Nor does it make a king."

He had blurred recollections of great wars taking place many years ago. High in the heavens where blood shed from both sides, as demons and angels collapsed under the fervent will of their respective rulers. The animosity sustained itself in the end, but a new enemy was now forged in the angel army.

"You'll see the sort of king I am right now!" Michael shouted.

Obelisk swung at Lycanthrope, breaking the air as it did so. The werewolf attempted to counter with its howling attack. Its counter fell on deaf ears just before taking the full force of the headless orc across the face.

Lycanthrope nearly collapsed from the pummeling blow. Shortly after, Tiamat came to its defense. The great vulture beat its wings to slow the headless orc down. Like a wall, Obelisk persisted. With its other fist, it struck Tiamat across the stomach. It squawked to the heavens in agony. Tiamat and Lycanthrope continued to berate their opposition with a myriad of attacks with few successful, for even they knew the hierarchy of titans could not be broken.

Lucifer stood there, watching both his servants take a vicious beating by Michael's titan. They grew bloodier by the second.

"Oh, I already have." He began. "I know just what sort of leader you are."

After several minutes passed, Lycanthrope and Tiamat stood beside one another, panting and screwing crimson on the ground. As it pooled through the grass, Obelisk stomped forward with a bellowing groan, as if preparing for its ultimate attack.

"You saw that potential when you made that proposition. Now, it's come back to bite you." Michael replied.

The serrated teeth within the headless orc's vortex of a cross-section spun like a turbine. Growing fast as the winds intensified.

"Obelisk, go. End this battle by wiping out both of his titans with your jowls of demise!"

Lucifer watched the new titan with despair as it grabbed both of the other titans with its glove-like hands.

Meanwhile, the strength seeped back into the girls. One

after the other, they creaked their eyes open, breaking from their unconsciousness and waking to the chaos.

"Michael. What is that?" Isabella mumbled. It must have been like some sort of dream to her, but to Lucifer, this was a petrifying reality. "What is that brute doing to my titans?"

"Your titans? You stole them from my friends. And when this is over, they'll be coming back to us. Now, my beast, feed upon these titans and rid my foe of his ambitions. With haste and without hesitation!"

"Outrageous! Those titans will never fit inside its mouth," said Lucifer.

"Let's find out," Michael said.

Lucifer trembled from Michael's unshakable confidence. "That'll never work. You fool!"

"You're forgetting Obelisk has other secret abilities."

"What other abilities?" Lucifer demanded.

"You'll see." Michael grinned.

The beast shoved both titans down its gullet-like shoulders, expanding its body like a giant balloon.

"That beast. It's about to"—

"That's right. It's about to combust," Michael finished. Obelisk could not devour both titans, no matter how hard it attempted to force them down his chasm-like gullet. It powered through anyway and exploded, taking the two titans down with it.

The vicious explosion left the battlefield shrouded in the guts and gore of the three dimensional titans.

"An angel? Able to summon a titan?"

He regained his composure and smiled.

"This was illuminating, to say the least. However, this means our convocation this evening is over. I must proceed to the next phase of my plan now. A plan that is guaranteed to succeed," Lucifer said to himself before backing into a blackened portal. Behind, its shadows resembled a void.

Michael called out to Lucifer. "Get back here and fight me, you coward," noticing Lucifer's exit.

"The entrails of the titans may return to their rings to be summoned again, but our war shall persist through any sea of blood."

"It'll continue right now!" Michael shouted.

"We'll meet again soon. And when we do, I assure you I won't be as merciful," Lucifer said with a grin before completely vanishing into the shadows.

CHAPTER 9
THE BEAST OF THE WETLANDS

Michael watched the manifestation of the void Lucifer's presence once filled, fixated and wondering when he'd next return.

You may have escaped this time, Lucifer, but you won't be so lucky the next time I see you. And I'm sure we will meet again.

Michael watched the last of the void vanish. He took a deep breath as the sun rose, before returning to his human form. With his original state came the disappearance of all the debris created by the explosion of the three titans.

He then turned around to see his friends limping up to their feet, in a fit of groans and winces.

"You guys? You're alright!"

He rushed to their aid with excitement and joy.

"Hey, did you see that? I scared that destroyer god straight back to the pit he crawled out of," said Michael with a hearty beam on his face. "On top of that, I have some exciting news about this vision I had and what it could mean."

The girls looked away from him, not with resentment or frustration, but with expressions of discomfort on their faces.

"You, know. You could act a little enthusiastic. I know I didn't kill him, but I think I scared him a bit. Also, did you see that titan I summoned out of nowhere?" he said, jumping with delight.

"Yes, we did, Michael," Julianna said with displeasure.

"Hey, is it something I said?" Michael said. "Are you still mad about me for not telling you earlier?"

"Get away from us!" Isabella snapped, cold as hail.

"There are bigger issues than you concealing his name from us," said Julianna.

"What do you mean? Did I do something wrong?" he wondered.

"I'll tell you what you did. You performed familiar magic," said Alexa.

"Yeah. And what's so wrong about that?" he asked.

The girls looked at each other, unsure of who should speak up next and how to approach the matter with him.

"Michael, only demons can perform familiar magic," Ursula said with concern in her voice.

"What?" Michael asked with bewilderment.

"Let me clarify," Alexa began, "familiar magic is the most forbidden and powerful form of magic to ever exist, and there's a reason for that. Only demons are granted the ability to perform it, as the darkness within them has evolved them to do."

"So, what are you saying?" Michael's lips quivered.

"I'm saying the archangel should be the last person who can perform such magic!" Alexa yelled.

"Okay. So, I performed demon magic. What's the big deal? It's not like I used it to hurt anyone who didn't deserve it," he argued.

"That's not the point, Michael. Only demons are granted the ability to use that magic. It's not that you shouldn't use that magic, it's that you shouldn't even be able to. Unless"—Julianna began.

"Unless what?" Michael said. The trembling in his voice grew.

"Unless you're actually a demon!" Ursula interjected.

Michael's eyes widened. It took every fiber of his being to maintain his composure in the face of the accusation. He looked at the distrusting gazes around him before taking a deep, calming breath.

"I see. You think I'm a demon because of the titan I summoned. I know that looked bad, but you know I'm not a demon. I'm an angel. The archangel and creator god, Michael. You have to believe me!"

"Throw around all the titles you want, Michael. Just answer this; how do we know you're not secretly working for Lucifer?" Julianna said.

"What? That's ridiculous. Where did that even come from?" Michael replied with astonishment.

"Well, for one, the fact you possess one of the seven titans. It only makes sense he lent you that one for this very purpose. To take us down," said Alexa.

"That's insane! You four are my friends," he said.

"He makes a good point. I've known him a long time and I don't think he'd be capable of something like that," Isabella interjected.

"I'd love to believe him so much," Julianna said with a sullen gaze.

"Then, believe me. Please," he said.

"But I have to know why you had that ring, and how you could use it, Michael," Julianna pressed.

"Guys, please." A cold sweat cascaded down Michael's shaking face. He felt the accusations weighing down and had no answers to lighten the burden. "I'm not"—

"I'm sorry, but this is all a bit too disconcerting for my taste," said Alexa.

"Would it help if I handed the ring over?" Michael dug into his pocket to reveal the ring. They all stepped back with cautious glares.

"I think the damage is already done, Michael," said Ursula.

The girls' made up their minds. They turned from him and walked away. Their abandonment of him brought tears to his eyes as his heart ached with remorse.

Michael would not give up just yet. He chased after them. "Where are you going?"

Alexa looked over her shoulder and said, "It's best we keep our distance for now. At least until we can figure out just the sort of person you are."

"The sort of person I am?" Michael recounted their evening by the campfire and the discussions they shared. "You know who I am."

"...but do you, Michael?" Alexa stopped in place. Looking over at Michael as he gulped nervously from her icy glare.

"Figure out why it is the archangel can use demonic magic and cast forth a titan thought to be in Lucifer's possession," Alexa continued.

"When you do, you can come and find us," Isabella added.

"But, you know the sort of person I am." Michael insisted.

Alexa took a deep breath. "I thought we did."

"I would never hurt you. Just listen."

Biting back her anguish, Alexa turned her attention forward before nodding. She didn't bother to look at him.

"Wait! You're all seriously leaving me behind?" Michael said.

"I'm sorry, Michael," Ursula said with a tear running down her cheek. The girls released their wings and flew away.

By the time the sun fully rose, Michael could no longer see them. They had completely disappeared. He dropped to his knees in disbelief.

"They left me all alone. No." In his mind, he could hear Lucifer's chuckling. It scratched at his mind like rusted nails.

"And it's all because I summoned that stupid fucking titan!" Michael smashed his fist into the ground.

Michael remembered the many days and nights he spent wandering his home village in the Dark Realm. They grew identical with each passing thought. The same scowls of derision from passersby. The same belligerent shouts from those who refused to welcome him and the same isolation he felt in his own home.

Tears rushed down his face. "I can't go back to who I was. I can't."

He recalled the day he slammed his fist against the glass and the blood that spilled from his fingers.

I haven't felt that way for even a moment. Not since I welcomed them all into my life with open arms.

Michael recalled the joyous days he spent capturing the elementals with Julianna, along with the day Isabella joined them on their mission. There were hardships, but their company made them easier.

Though his time with Alexa and Ursula was far shorter, one of his happiest moments was healing their broken bonds because he saw much of himself in them. So much of his loneliness and desperation. Now, it was all he had.

"I should have treated them better. I should have listened when they asked me to train. I should have been more open about my feelings."

He recalled each morning they woke him up. He would roll towards the other side with a groan, still smiling with the presence of someone by his side. Someone who cared.

All they wanted was the best out of me. They even went out of their way to help me when I drank my potion. And I repay them by using demon magic?

Michael struck his fist down at the nearest rock. Blood spilled just as it did that day against the glass.

And now I'm back to where I started. But why do I feel even worse?

His mind raced with the visions he saw of that familiar estate. The sight of him calling forth a titan he'd never seen locked in. He soon began to question it all. What it meant and how he came to know all this. And how he forgot it.

Just who the fuck am I?

He looked up at the beating sun and screamed out of rage.

I'm alone. More than ever before because the person I am is becoming almost impossible to recognize.

Michael curled up in a ball as memories of his childhood flooded in. The memories of his adoptive parents beating him. The shouting he received from Isabella. And the world's refusal to let him in.

Why does this keep happening? Is this what fate has for me? Eternal solitude? That can't be all I have to live for!

He laughed to himself, shaking his head.

I won't give up that easily. Not this time. I won't seek solace at the end of a liquor bottle. I'll earn back their trust if it's the last thing I do.

He rose to his feet and dusted himself off. He looked into the direction the girls flew—into the woods ahead of the open fields.

The golden horizon hanging over the branches was as warm as the surrounding winds were cold.

His wings were strained from the battle, so he knew it was best to get started before the sun set again, fully aware of how long it could take to find them.

Whatever it takes, no matter how much I need to beg, I'll find a way to get back in their good graces.

He took the little he had on him and walked towards the direction in which they flew, hoping they had made no turns.

THE GIRLS ADVANCED INTO THE WOODS, ENTERING A murky swamp-like region with pools of water around and branches hanging inside. Trees echoed with the croaking of frogs and the groaning of alligators. The pungent scent of the swamp filled the air, making their stomachs churn.

"Was it a good idea to leave him behind? I don't think there was any malcontent behind summoning that titan," Ursula said. She recalled the sincere look on his face before they left him. She choked on her tears as more sympathy built in her.

"You're probably right. I think that innocent and somewhat dimwitted side of him will always be there," said Julianna.

"But this whole being a god and twin brother ordeal will take a lot of time digesting. As will his connection to that titan," said Alexa.

"It's not like it's his fault," Ursula began. "He learned about this just as we did."

"Assuming that's even true, that doesn't explain where he got that titan," Julianna said.

The squelching of the swamp under their feet attracted the attention of a denizen—far larger than an alligator—lurking in the muddy swamp. Its yellow eyes glared at the oblivious girls as a jagged grin formed across its face.

"How do you think he got it, though?" Isabella asked.

"It's possible he stole the ring and just forgot about it," said Alexa.

"Normally, I'd scoff at such a suggestion, but he is a pretty heavy drinker. Maybe it's true that he forgot," Isabella said.

"What I know is he's the last person who'd ever hurt us." Julianna recounted his battles with Ursula and Alexa. "He makes enough mistakes for any lifetime, but he isn't a bad person and you know that."

Alexa took a deep breath. "I know. It was just a lot to take in."

"So, you're not mad at him?" Ursula's eyes glowed with hope.

❦

ALEXA RECALLED THE NIGHT PRIOR WHEN DINNER CAME TO a close, then she and the girls got to their share of work on the dishes.

"I can't believe how many servings this one guy can finish," she groaned.

She looked over her shoulder, turning to where she last saw him.

"Hey, if it's not too much trouble for the archangel, do you mind cleaning your damn dishes"—

She saw him sleeping on the ground with a blanket wrapped around him. He rolled back and forth, mumbling under his breath. He said her name and the rest of his friends' with a smile on his face. The frustration she felt melted with the warmth of his simple words. Like watching a child rest, Alexa smiled too.

❦

"A LITTLE, STILL, BUT I'LL GET OVER IT." ALEXA SMILED. "AS you all said, he's not a bad person. He's just a dumbass."

"Wait, when did any of us say that last part?" Ursula asked.

Alexa dismissed the question with a smirk. "Let's say we gather a few provisions—meat and wood, perhaps—and make a nice dinner as a way of apologizing and for thanking him for dinner last night."

"That's a great idea," Ursula exclaimed.

They all nodded in agreement, and then walked in opposite directions, scouring the swamplands for branches and wild boars.

Ursula strayed away from the group with a certainty that she heard a squeal. "Come on, little piggy. Where are you?" She followed the roots of a tree and tripped over one of them.

The rest of the girls heard the thump in the distance and ran in her direction.

"Ursula, are you alright?" Alexa asked.

"I'll be fine." Sore from the fall, Ursula rose to her feet and noticed a scrape on her knee.

"You're injured. Let me help." Isabella walked towards her with a healing spell prepared in her hands.

"Thanks." Alexa and Julianna held her up as Isabella performed the remedy.

"How did you fall, anyway?" Alexa asked.

"This tree root just came out of nowhere," Ursula said.

"Why does that excuse sound familiar?" Alexa said with a dim eyed glare.

"I'm serious. Look down."

Puzzled, she and the others looked at the web of roots on the ground. They noticed a sickly pink one among the earthy shades.

Alexa nervously gulped as she watched it squirm.

"Ursula."

"Yes?"

"That's not a fucking root!"

They all dispersed with panic and confusion, but it was too late. The deceptive vein among the tree roots had captured them.

THEIR SCREAMS BULLETED ACROSS THE FOREST AND Michael received them. His heart thundered with terror.

"Shit! That was them!"

He ran with haste, following the sounds of their cries, jumping over ponds and ducking below the rotting logs.

They're in danger. Something got them. I know it!

He dove through the vines and trees. Over the many scum-covered ponds and mossy stones, along with a wooden sign that said: "Beware of the jagged distortion that resides here. In the wetlands of *Mgla*, all shall be consumed."

As Michael ran, he noticed his surroundings change. The trees grew emaciated and caves emerged from the weeping shadows, all splattered with blood that trickled into the mud-ridden waters.

His heart beat faster. He hardly noticed the bloodstains or the mounds of animal and human remains hanging and laid around him.

Making his way deeper, the sound of a roar left him frozen in place. He peered into the water and saw an alligator rise. It stared in his direction with glowing yellow eyes. His heart pounded as the alligator's jaws crept open.

Why do I always have to run into wild animals? Why can't I just walk into a forest in peace for once?

Michael panted as the alligator slithered towards him. He prepared himself to summon his scepter as a defense when he felt a tugging at his feet. Frightened, he looked down. The mud grew so thick and potent; it pulled him down like sticky quicksand.

He attempted to break free with his lightning, but the mud absorbed his strikes. "Damn it!"

He gritted his teeth as he reached for the surrounding

branches, but they were too far away now that he was sinking deeper.

More than halfway into the ground, he looked up at the menacing glare of the beast just a few feet away. He saw the carcass of the last animal it ate. Its bones hung from its jaw.

"Nice alligator. I promise I'll get out of your swamp and be on my way. As soon I can figure a way out of here."

Michael sank deeper into the swamp's depths as the alligator grew closer. Wisps of its fiery breath flared from its nostrils onto Michael's face. He looked away in despair.

I need to get out of here fast. Even if they don't want my help or even want to see me again, I owe them that much. And I owe it to myself, too, to get back the only people that have ever been there for me!

With a vicious grunt, he took one last chance at grabbing the vine nearest to him. Before he could, the alligator lunged at it and broke it with its jaws.

"Of course you just did that. Fantastic!"

Michael closed his eyes as the alligator prepared to pounce when only his head was left sticking out from the ground. Michael expected the alligator to eat him alive right then, but instead, the roar of another beast met him. He creaked one eye open to the sight of a massive tentacle clutching alligator.

"What the fuck was that?!"

Michael looked around and only registered now he was stuck in a bog of rotting flesh. Countless boars, rabbits, cattle, and many other beasts hanged from the trees and scattered through the ponds and grounds—mutilated, as the buzzards picked at their remains. He concluded that whatever yanked him out was the culprit behind all the carcasses.

The last of him began to sink into the mud. He closed his eyes, accepting fate when a massive hand pulled him straight out.

Gasping for air, he turned around with bewilderment. He was thankful to be alive but still wondered what just grabbed him.

Michael looked down at the furry pink slug-like exterior, gazing into its horrific golden stare, knowing he was better off underground.

The beast threw him towards the ground and he landed in a very open region of the swamp. He then looked forward, seeing an abomination of jagged clawed arms on either side, with tendril tongues pouring from its gaping jaws. It had the most hideous face he'd ever seen. Distorted past his understanding, its jaws spread throughout what resembled a head.

Its teeth glistened like a bottomless chasm of spikes. The trees corroded as it salivated all around the swamp like the savage slob it was. The tentacles emerging from its mouth and arms were especially deplorable. With antler-like horns and a single eye to top off its grotesque appearance, it was like something from another world.

As if broken from the trance placed by the creature's revolting appearance, Michael heard the screams of his friends. His eyes immediately widened as he saw the beast carrying them in its tentacles.

"Ursula, Isabella, Julianna, and Alexa."

"What the hell are you doing here?" Isabella asked, struggling to break the creature's grip.

"Saving you. Even if you don't want my help, you've got it. Always."

Julianna looked at the others with a smile, knowing the decision to trust him all along was right.

"In that case, hurry your ass up."

"Our weapons fell when this beast grabbed us." Isabella eyed the pile of swords, a mallet, and an ax laying by the tree.

"And this beast's grip is too tight for us to use our magic,"

Ursula said, feeling her arms tightened under the coiling grip of the swamp beast.

The tentacle holding her craned towards the beast's jaws as they slowly opened. Alexa watched in defeat as a screaming Ursula inched towards its mouth.

"Ursula!"

Michael's rage grew from the very sight.

"That's it. This ugly fucker's finished!"

He immediately transformed into his etherial state. He cast his scepter by his side and released his wings. In the blink of an eye, he rushed towards the four of them and slashed through the tentacles holding them, releasing them from the beast's grip. They safely thudded onto the ground before the bleeding creature sprayed them with its puss.

"Michael, you saved us!" Ursula hugged him tightly with a smile.

"Not yet," Michael replied, catching his breath. He looked up at the hulking creature. It roared with fury as its tentacles slowly grew back. "I still need to make sure this beast is over with."

The girls nervously gulped, stepping back. Michael spread his feet apart and raised his staff in a horizontal position, and then voltage emanated from his fingertips. It shocked and lit up brighter until he could no longer contain it.

"Go! Electric burst!"

Bolts of lightning rushed from his scepter and into the water, electrocuting the beast. The beast roared as it blackened to ash. With a final groan, it collapsed into the water, unleashing a tidal wave that soaked them all.

Michael watched the creature sink in the swamp. He took a deep breath, preparing to approach his friends.

When he walked over to them, he saw wandering gazes of embarrassment on their faces.

"We could have done that ourselves, you know," Alexa said, pouting.

"I know you could. I did it to say thanks."

The girls looked at him, confused.

"Thanks for what?" Isabella asked.

"We're the ones that left you behind," said Ursula.

"Thanks for being my friend. Even if you don't know if you can trust me yet, I'll do everything in my power to earn it."

"Michael. We"—Alexa began.

"I know my still missing memories will be a pain for us all as I learn more of who I used to be, and how I got that titan in the first place. But I won't let that get in the way of who I want to be right now: someone who cares deeply for his friends. So, if you'd be alright giving me another chance"—

"Yes, Michael."

Julianna's swift response took him by surprise. "Wait, you mean that?"

"Don't get it twisted. I think we're all pretty annoyed you didn't tell us about meeting Lucifer before," Alexa said.

"Right." Michael looked down, downhearted.

"And we still don't know how you summoned or got that titan in the first place," Isabella added.

"Yeah. That, too. Look, I"—

"But, you're nothing like your brother outside of his face. Your selflessness proves that much," said Alexa.

"No matter what you learn about yourself, you'll still be you. And well, we like you a lot," Ursula said with a smile.

Their smiles and sincere words they brought stunned him. He shook in place and succumbed to emotions.

"I don't know what to say. Just thank you so much."

"Don't cry." Ursula wiped his tears away.

"And don't keep secret from us, either. Understand?" Alexa said.

"Yes." Michael nodded with a smile. He then remembered the vision he had back in the estate. "Now that you mention it, there is something really important I'd like to tell you all if that's alright."

"Please do, Michael," Julianna said.

Michael smiled and nodded, then recounted his vision during the battle with Lucifer. From the very beginning, when he walked through the bazaars like a ghost, to the strong bond he felt in the estate. He told them about the darkened figures he saw—how they seemed rather familiar and how they appeared to be watching him, the understanding during the fall he had that everything he saw and felt were fragments of who he was, waiting to be put together.

"What do you think?" Michael asked.

The four of them looked at one another in silence before smiling.

"You have an interesting imagination." Julianna laughed. They joined her in laughter.

"But it sounds like you've made some major progress in figuring out who you were. For that, I'm proud of you." Isabella smiled.

"And for the first time in a while, I actually can't wait to have another dream," Michael said.

"Just be sure not to go drinking before bed—or at all, if you can help it," said Alexa. They all laughed and nodded.

"I'll do my best."

"Good. Now, let's get the hell out of this swamp before another beast appears and tries to consume us," said Julianna. "It's still a while before sundown, but I don't want to take my chances."

"Speaking of which, how about the four of us make dinner tonight?" Alexa said.

Michael's eyes widened. "Really? You don't have to if"—

"We'd be happy to," Julianna insisted.

"But you have to clean up," Ursula said.

"That hardly seems fair." Michael sighed before smiling. "Even so, I'd be happy to."

"Then, let's go. I'm starving for some boar," said Alexa.

The others nodded.

Together, the five of them released their wings and took to the sky, flying over the swamplands. They were bound for their campsite, ready to celebrate their evening of reconciliation with a freshly roasted meal.

CHAPTER 10
THE MECHANICAL WITCH

The following morning, Michael creaked open his eyes to the rays of the morning sun beaming into his tent, flustered by the staining sensation. He wondered how early it was, feeling a slight aching in his head.

This ordeal of maintaining sobriety and not sleeping through the mornings won't be easy, he thought.

He looked down, thinking he was in some sort of dream. He found the girls gathered in his tent, all wrapped around him—dressed in hardly any clothes, with smiles on their faces.

What the hell are they all doing here?

Michael's eyes scanned every corner of the tent in search of their clothes.

I know we made up and everything during dinner last night.

Michael recalled the night laughter they all shared during dinner: from cooking together to telling many stories. They all wore elated smiles as they basked one another's company.

I was so relieved to be back with them again. My friends.

Their grip around him tightened. His face turning blue,

he inched his fingers out from under them. The clinginess seemed a bit too much to him.

As he tried to get up, Julianna and Alexa dragged him back onto the floor.

Michael realized that even in their sleep, they wouldn't let go, feeling their collective grip tighten. He looked for another way out.

I know. I'll slowly slide through.

He tried to slip through the girls, slithering like a caterpillar. After a few inches of progress, a tugging on his pants stopped him. It was Isabella pulling his pants off with a wide grin and a giggle.

Well, I knew I wouldn't make it out of here with my clothes, but as long as I can make it out at all, I should be fine.

Michael persisted in trying to slip past them. He then felt a kissing sensation on his leg. He looked down, found out it was Ursula's touch this time. She grabbed on, moving farther up his leg than he could keep up.

What's come over them? Not that I mind. Embarrassment filled Michael. He drooled from the many hands and lips latching on.

He could feel his heart pounding out of his chest and his blood rushing when Alexa dragged him down, burying his face between her breasts.

"You're not going anywhere," Alexa said with a playful smile.

"You're awake?" Michael's face turned blue from the suffocating grip.

"Of course. We all are. We just like watching you squirm a bit," Alexa said, holding tighter.

The others opened their eyes. They wiped out their smiles and gasped at Michael's face going from blue to purple.

"Hey, you're hurting him," Julianna said, mulled at his arms.

"No, I wasn't. If he had a problem with getting a face full of breasts in the morning, then he wouldn't be pitching a second tent by Ursula's face," said Alexa.

"I think she means he can't breathe," Ursula said, who noticed his tent drooping.

Alexa looked down at Michael's face, which had now gone completely purple. "Oh, no. You're right!" She swiftly released her grip on him.

"I'm so sorry. Are you alright?" she continued, shaking him back and forth.

"Just peachy," Michael said, as he felt his head spin across the room with four sets of eyes staring back at him.

He caught his breath as his face returned to form and then looked over at their nervous faces with a groan.

"I appreciate the affection in the morning, but do you mind not sneaking into my tent when I'm still asleep?" Michael suggested.

"Sorry. It was Alexa's idea," Ursula said.

"Hey!" Alexa groaned. "You and your big mouth."

"Wait, you decided to do this?" Michael asked, perplexed.

Alexa sighed and nodded. "Isabella told me a bit more about your struggle last night."

"You mean after the fire?"

Michael vaguely recalled heading to bed and seeing the two of them converse by the dwindling fire, staring at one another with concern in their eyes.

"By the sounds of what I heard, I assumed quitting wouldn't be so easy. So I thought you could use some motivation," said Alexa.

"Instead of waking up with a hangover, how about four women by your side?" Julianna said.

"And all you have to do is refrain from drinking," Isabella said with a smile.

Michael looked down at his blanket. Feeling a sensation

rise as they gathered closer, he smiled. "I think that could work."

The girls responded with a laugh.

"Let's hope so," said Alexa.

"Now that I'm up, what's on the schedule?" Michael asked.

"Training. Lots and lots of training," said Julianna.

"I see," said Michael. "We should be better prepared next time Lucifer strikes."

"Exactly," Ursula said, recalling their entrapment and his robbery of their rings. The helplessness she felt ate at her. "So, hurry. We all need to get in top fighting shape. Especially you, Michael."

"Sounds like a plan." Michael nodded with a smile. As he tried to get up, he felt a sharp jolt in his pants.

"How about you girls get a head start? I'll meet you guys in about thirty minutes."

Alexa sighed. "Thirty minutes? Please try to be more discreet with your plans."

"Yes, we all know what thirty minutes means," Julianna said with a devious grin.

Michael blushed. "Now, I think I could use a drink."

"Calm down. I was kidding. Just get dressed," said Alexa.

"Alright," Michael said with reluctance in his voice.

He got out of his tent to the clanking of swords outside, dressed and ready after forty-five minutes. He looked around and spotted the girls sparring. A sense of warmth filled him, knowing the semblance of his new normal prevailed through the panic of the last few days. His old and new friends trained together in harmony, and he had the chance to be a part of it. He walked towards them with a smile.

"Sticking to the same weapon, I see."

He walked towards them, amazed by the swift and

scrupulous movements they made almost effortlessly with their blades.

"Indeed. We believe doing so will prove to be the most efficient way of gauging our individual strengths," said Julianna.

"As if. You clearly have an advantage over the rest of us. You just want to look good in his presence," said Isabella.

"And what's wrong with that? It's not my fault I'm the only one trained in the art of sword fighting," Julianna said, unapologetically.

Alexa rolled her eyes and walked to the side. She placed her sword to her side and pulled out a device from her pocket.

"Hey, where are you going?" Isabella asked.

"Nowhere. Just reading something."

She scrolled through the screen with her fingers, reading virtual news articles. The others swarmed around with intrigue.

"Unholy shit; there are words on that thing," Isabella said.

"It's called a screen and yes. You have a lot to learn about steam technology," Alexa stated.

"I suppose so," Isabella said with widened eyes.

Alexa continued to sift through various articles, twitching with frustration as they all continued to loom over her shoulders.

"Have you found anything interesting? Perhaps something on magic restrictions in a certain forest being lifted?" Ursula asked with a hopeful smile.

"Fat chance of that," Julianna said.

Alexa stopped scrolling and froze in place. She quivered in disbelief as her hand shook out of control.

"Is everything alright?" Michael asked.

"You tell me," said Alexa, handing Isabella her device.

"It's a news article," Alexa began, "Clockwork Designs declares bankruptcy, falling to the new ownership of"—

Terrified, Ursula snatched the device from her hand to read it herself. She gasped at the name on the screen.

"Lucifer Morningstar? This must be some kind of joke!"

"I'm afraid it's not. I don't know how he did it, but that snake bought my company from under me," Alexa said.

"Are you sure you're reading that right?" Michael asked.

"I am," Alexa replied in a sullen tone. "The Steam Gazette is the most trustworthy resource in my home dimension."

"I don't know how things work in your homeland, but don't you have to approve a buyout before it can happen?" Julianna suggested.

"I guess when you're as conniving as the demon king, you can work your way around such restraints," Alexa replied.

"You really think so?" Isabella suggested.

"I don't have any explanation. Just that my money's gone," Alexa said with a tremble in her voice.

"That's terrible. Just when you thought he couldn't sink any lower!" Julianna shouted.

"I don't think he forgot you guys, either." Ursula continued, pulling up the other tabs on the device.

Isabella and Julianna looked at the headlines in shock.

"No way, my jewelry company," Isabella lamented.

"...and my sword company," Julianna added.

"All bought out," said Alexa.

"Oh, no. Does this mean?" Ursula began.

"Yes," Alexa replied. "This means we don't have a single gold piece to our names. That prick cleaned us all out."

"He even liquidated my lizard farm in the first dimension. How could he? That was my only source of income!" Ursula shouted.

How could this have happened? Michael thought as he watched his friends grieving. Unaware of a shadow looming over them. He then remembered what Lucifer said about his plundering magic. "That's it!"

"What's it?" Alexa asked.

"I know how Lucifer did it. His plundering magic. It allows him to steal whatever he wants. That's how he took your companies and money. I'm so sorry," Michael said.

"That belligerent cunt!" Alexa shouted. "Just how low is he willing to go?"

"I didn't think he could get much lower than beating an innocent young girl," Ursula said, remembering her conversation with Julianna after dinner the night prior. She broke down into tears as she went through the memories. "No. He just has to ruin everything around him when he doesn't get his way. Fuck this guy!"

"He'll pay for this. The next time we met, he's dead! Do you hear me?" Alexa shouted to the sky. "No one crosses the queen of the sixth dimensions and gets away with it!"

"Why is he even doing this? Is it simply because we're allied with his enemy?" Isabella suggested.

I'm sure he's been planning this ever since he evaded our last encounter, Michael thought with a sneer as he remembered him leaving into his portal.

He's callous but shrewd. He knows how to use every piece on the battlefield to his advantage. Even the ones that aren't his own.

He recalled their chess game—how his pieces slowly diminished as the game progressed, and those of his opponent. The disregard in Lucifer's moves proved clearer with his latest action.

Tears flowed down Michael's face as he watched them run down Ursula's. He then remembered something he found.

"Here." Michael dug into his pocket, revealing a small golden orb.

"What's that?" Ursula asked.

"It's the core of the beast I slew in the swamp the other day. Sell it."

"Sell it?" Isabella asked.

"I don't know how much it'll be worth, but it should last long enough for us to sort this out," Michael replied.

"Michael?" Alexa's eyes widened. Teary now from the gesture. "You don't have to."

"Yeah, that's your money," Isabella insisted.

"It's fine." Michael smiled. "I can always make money some other way. Maybe hunting livestock or chopping wood."

His unbridled kindness swept them away and left them lost for words. They simply let their tears trickle down.

Julianna took a deep breath and picked the core from his hand. "Thank you, Michael. But we can't sell it."

"Why not?" Michael asked.

"Because it's a gift from you," Julianna said. "We could never part ways with it."

The other girls looked at one another, nodding with the sentiment.

"She's right. It's way too precious. Also, it carries the memories of when you saved of in that swamp," said Ursula.

"And were we reconciled," Isabella said with a smile.

"Are you sure?" Michael's eyes widened, taken by both the tenderness in their eyes and the sincerity they carried.

"Besides, we could use it in our future battles," said Alexa.

Michael watched the solemn expressions on their faces and nodded.

"Alright, if that's your choice, then it looks like we should get busy taking on quests to raise the money we need."

The girls nodded in agreement. Suddenly, Ursula's infinity bag began to glow.

"Hey, what's going on?" She looked inside and saw a flashing light.

"That means you've received a parcel or mail," Julianna said.

"Really?"

Suddenly, everyone else's infinity bags began to glow. They opened up their bags to see what awaited them. Inside them were small books, identical in appearance.

"Gaming manuals?" Michael wondered, reading through his copy.

"*To Eve the Art of Witchcraft*. By Lucifer Morningstar." Julianna read the cover with a disdainful look.

"Just what is he up to now?" Isabella said.

"It looked like he sent out a copy to every black magic user across the omniverse," Alexa said, scrolling through a long list of recipients.

"These appear to be new battle regulations on how to fight in formal battles," said Isabella.

"Fuck that shit. I'm not following his dumb rules," Ursula declared, crossing her arms in defiance.

"Sounds like the first piece of good news we've heard from him," said Julianna.

"How do you figure that?" Ursula asked.

"Simple. Because now we are on the same playing field as his," Julianna replied with a grin.

They all looked at her, realizing her point.

"That's right. If we have to follow these same rules, so does he, right?" Michael asked, remembering the various games he played with him in his dream.

"Yes, and by the looks of it, there are many," Isabella said, skimming through the book.

"Indeed. Witchcraft, as a game, seems rather complex. For one, we have to maintain a certain number of terrains on the battlefield if we want to perform certain spells," Alexa said.

"Terrains? What does that mean?" Ursula asked.

"Places like jungles and oceans. Seems you can call them forth much like you can familiars," Alexa said.

"You mean you can summon an ocean?" Ursula's eyes widened.

"It says here the number of terrains we have is determined by the number of turns we take in battle," she explained.

"So, we're battling on a turn basis?" Julianna groaned.

"Yes, and the terrains become part of an entity called the landscape." Said Isabella. "The larger your landscape is, the more familiars you can summon."

"This game sounds kind of fun. It says here the more terrain a familiar needs, the more powerful it is," Michael said.

"It also says some familiars require a sacrifice of other familiars, too, because they're so powerful," said Ursula.

They all looked down at the orb.

"I wonder how powerful this one is," said Isabella.

"Let's find out," Alexa said, scanning it with her device. "*Xendrazi*, the jagged distortion. A monarch class familiar."

"There are different classes of familiars?" Michael asked.

"Yes, and by the looks of it, monarch is a pretty high class. Albeit, not as high as titan," Alexa said.

"Great!" he said, enthusiastically.

"Not exactly," Alexa replied as she continued reading.

"Huh? What do you mean?"

"Apparently, if you want to summon a beast like this in battle, it'll prove quite costly."

"Costly how?" he replied with a nervous gulp.

"From what I gather here, a monarch type familiar requires four terrains and two other familiars."

"Two other familiars? Just for this one?" Ursula's eyes widened.

"Seems servant class familiars are best to use as a sacrifice, as they are the easiest to bring out and the weakest," Alexa suggested.

"But, what good is all this information when titans and this monarch are the only familiars we have in our possession?" Isabella asked.

"So, you're saying we can't even use it?" he asked.

"I'm afraid not. And looking through here, it seems titans are even tougher to use. Seven terrains and five sacrifices. Ridiculous," Alexa said as irritation grew in her.

"No kidding. So, we can't even use our best familiars?" Michael said, realizing Lucifer's underhandedness in the rules of the game he crafted.

"We can still cast enchantments, however. They cost terrain, as well. They can be used to protect us in battle," said Isabella, reading her manual.

Michael took a sigh of relief. "Better than nothing, I suppose."

"However, it's highly recommended to use familiars in battle, as they are the central focus of the game," Ursula read out.

The girls looked at her at once, realizing how difficult this game would become for them and what that would mean in challenging Lucifer again.

"If that's the case, I wonder what sort of familiars Lucifer has in his possession. If he's creating this game, he must have some powerful ones at his disposal, and some weaker ones to bring them out," said Julianna.

"So much for an equal playing field," Isabella said, downhearted.

"Hey, don't get so down. We can still do this," said Michael.

"How? He's clearly rigged this from the start!" Alexa fumed.

"That's not true. Familiars or not, he's only as strong now

as his terrain count will allow. We just need to find some weaker familiars to help bring out our heavyweights, while also mastering spells that debilitate his landscape. Then, we'll smash his stupid face in," Michael said with a confident grin.

"You make it sound so easy," Ursula said, warming up to the idea, but still unsure if it wielded any credibility.

"And what makes you think he won't cheat?" Julianna asked.

"That's a good point," Isabella began, "Lucifer's a dirty snake. Regardless of how the battle goes, I bet he'll still try to pull a fast one on us."

"I'm not saying it will be easy. I'm saying victory is there for us if we want it. We just have to work hard and believe. And as for whether he plans to cheat, let's just say I've found in my own way he's a man of integrity in games. I doubt he or anyone else could cheat, even if they wanted to," said Michael.

"Anyone else? I forgot other members of his legion may be after us." Ursula slumped into an anguished state.

"Their familiars will most likely be very powerful, as well, given their ties to the creator of the game," said Alexa.

Creator, Michael thought.

"Whatever the obstacle, we can face it together. We may have the disadvantage, but I still believe with the right amount of teamwork, we can conquer whatever adversaries come our way."

"You know how to rally the troops. I like that in a leader. I'm in," said Julianna.

"Me, too. Besides. I want to see that look on that destroyer jackass's face when we take back everything that he took from us and so much more," said Isabella.

The four of them smiled and nodded.

"Me, three. Especially if Michael will be there every step of the way to support us," said Ursula.

They all now focused their looks at Alexa as she looked off to the side. She sighed with a smile.

"Very well. If you're all in, so am I."

"Then, it's settled. We'll beat Lucifer at his own game, using the very titans he seeks to gather," said Michael.

"And get our money back!" Alexa chanted.

The five of them placed their hands together in a circle, ready to raise them high towards the sky when quaking below their feet broke the mood. A thunderous noise threw them into a sudden panic.

"What's going on? Some sort of earthquake?" Ursula exclaimed over the sounds of the ground cracking wide.

"I don't think so. This feels different, somehow," Michael said, analyzing the strange sensation he felt.

Out from the ground rose a strange figure clad in robes, a blackened mask, and a pointed hat. Female in physique with a shadow complexion, the figure stared directly at Michael and the girls, as they all stood there, completely frozen—baffled.

"Is that a witch?" Isabella gazed at the unusual female figure and the aura she gave off, sensing a demonic presence.

"Seems so, but where did she come from?" Alexa asked.

"That's the work of Lucifer," Michael announced.

"How can you tell?" Isabella asked.

"The energy emitting from her. It's the same as Lucifer's," said Michael.

They looked towards the witch's face and only saw a swirling stream of shadows where it would be.

The skies darkened too, forging a sweeping tempest of writhing clouds hanging over them. They gazed, petrified, as gusts of fire rolled and hurdled through the thundering heavens.

"Entering witchcraft sequence. Battle will now commence," the witch said in an eerie, unsettling tone. Like a machine, she raised her arms with a creaking movement of gears in each joint.

"I see. It's an android." Alexa immediately recognized the dreary tone she'd heard many times from her home dimension.

"Android? What's that?" Isabella said, her eyes fixated at the witch, as well.

"They're mechanical creatures with human appearances, usually designed to serve the bidding of others," Alexa replied.

"In that case, I think Michael may have been right," said Isabella, "This is Lucifer's doing."

"He doesn't waste any time, does he?" Julianna said.

Stealing their companies and now sicking this mechanical witch on us, Michael thought as his eyes dimmed. *Now, he's moving his pieces in.*

"First turn commence. Casting one dark terrain," the witch said as a massive blackened wasteland appeared, scorching a portion of the open field.

"You're right. But who should battle her?" Isabella asked as the girls exchanged looks.

Michael took a deep breath and stepped forward. "I'll do it."

"You?" the girls asked in unison.

"Is that honestly a good idea?" Julianna asked.

"I know you can summon a titan, but angels shouldn't be getting involved in things like this," Ursula said.

"Yeah, I know. The reality is I can use familiar magic. I don't know how. I just know that if I don't use my abilities to their fullest, they'll be wasted. So let me do this, please. He is after me."

They all reluctantly nodded.

"Fine. I just hope you know what you're doing," said Alexa.

"I'll be fine. I've played Lucifer's games before," Michael said while approaching the witch so they were about twenty feet apart and facing one another.

Knowing his integrity in games from experience, I smell a rat, Alexa thought to herself.

The witch looked back at Michael through shadowy fixtures, as he stared at her with confidence. "Proceeding to harnessing phase."

"Harnessing?" Michael wondered.

"Harnessing one dark terrain to cast orc gathering grounds."

"Did you say orcs?" Michael stepped back with dread. Soon, a large cave similar to what he saw in his nightmares emerged from the ground.

"Did you see that? She just manifested a cave from the ground," Ursula said. The others stared, baffled.

"Activating enchantment's ability. By casting three angel spawn to opponent's field, cast one orc onto mine," said the witch.

"I beg your pardon?"

Suddenly, three grotesque puppet-like angels rose onto Michael's side of the battlefield. He looked at them, overwhelmed with confusion.

"You're giving me three familiars?"

"What a weird move. The witch starts by giving her opponent a huge lead," said Isabella.

"Not as huge as she wants you to think. Don't forget that was a cost to be paid for her actual intentions," said Julianna.

"She's right. We're about to see firsthand just how fierce a game of witchcraft can really be," said Alexa.

"I suppose there's more to this game than we thought," Ursula closed.

"Three angel spawn cast. Now casting orc." From the cave emerged a hulking purple figure with wet jet-black hair, disheveled and partially covering its war-torn face and blood-red eyes.

Michael stared up at the beast, utterly mortified. *That beast is just like the one in my nightmare.*

He vividly recalled the circle of beasts that surrounded him in his dream long ago and the black dragon that ended it all.

"Don't give up, Michael! It just looks bad because it's so much bigger and stronger looking than your angels," Ursula chanted.

"Thanks," Michael replied, left now to further acknowledge the blatant size difference between his familiars and the witch's. The wire-like flies caught in the web of a towering spider. And he was part of its prey.

"Familiars cannot attack the turn I summon them. Ending turn," said the witch.

Michael took a sigh of relief. "Good. I was worried for a second there."

"You may want to keep worrying," Alexa said, looking through her device.

"Why? Is something wrong?" Ursula asked.

"Yeah. That orc enchantment of hers. There's a nasty side effect to having those angels. If Michael doesn't attack with them, they're destroyed at the end of the turn and he takes something called 'trample damage'."

"That doesn't sound good." Isabella gulped.

"It isn't," Alexa replied as she continued to read through the pages of her book. "It's like having the familiar's life-force drained from you."

"Oh, no!" said the other girls in unison.

"But Michael can't attack with those angels. They're too weak to survive," said Isabella.

"He'll just have to be more creative, it seems. Find a way

to get around that spell," Julianna said, looking carefully at Michael.

Michael took a deep breath. "My turn. I cast a light terrain." The fledgling sun drowning among the black sky above grew brighter as the clouds ceded to its presence. "Then, I attack with all of my angel spawn."

"You what?" Alexa asked in disbelief.

The puppet-like angels raised their scepters, crashing into the orcs. The orcs mercilessly slew each one of them with the crushing force of their fists.

Michael looked on as the smoke cleared, finding his side of the battlefield empty in a matter of moments. He kept an unphased expression despite his losses—staring blankly towards the witch.

"Why the hell did he do that?" Ursula exclaimed. "He has no forces left.

"And because he doesn't have to take trample damage at the end of the turn," said Isabella.

"That was quick thinking," Alexa said. "He evaded the detriments of having them on his battlefield. However, with them gone, he's at the mercy of a direct attack from that orc."

"If this is the work of Lucifer, he's giving us one hell of a crash course on how this game works," said Julianna.

"Turn two commence. Casting second dark terrain and unharnessing first terrain," said the witch, as the wastelands grew.

"Unharnessing?" Ursula asked. "What does that mean?"

"That's another condition of this game, it seems," Alexa began, "All harnessed lands unharness themselves at the beginning of each turn, making them reusable."

"Which doesn't bode well for Michael since it isn't his turn any longer," said Julianna.

"Act-vating ability of orc battling ground. Now doubling forces."

With the mechanical witch's words, a second orc emerged from the cave, groaning and swinging his bat as its flesh became exposed to the light.

"Second ability of enchantment. Cast three angel spawn onto opponent's side of the battlefield."

Three angel spawn appeared before Michael, just as before. He stared at them nervously.

"A second orc, already? This hardly seems right," Julianna said.

"What do you mean?" Ursula asked.

"Orcs are powerful creatures. I know that from stories I've heard. Based on that, they shouldn't be this easy to cast," said Julianna.

"She's right," said Alexa, looking over at the witch. "Orcs are some of the mightiest beasts to hail from the third dimension. Yet, this witch casts them forth without a second thought for hardly any cost."

"What are you implying here?" Isabella wondered.

"I think there's some serious cheating going on."

She and the girls looked over at Michael, who tried his best to shroud his fear under a smile.

"Poor Michael," Ursula said.

"Initiating battle sequence. Orc one, attack angel spawn one," the witch commanded. The orc charged towards the left-most angel spawn with a decorous roar.

"This is it. I wonder if Michael can stop that witch's attack," said Alexa.

"You think he can?" Isabella asked.

"He has a terrain he didn't harness in his last turn for whatever reason. Perhaps he was waiting to use it for the right moment."

"I see. So, we can use terrains during either person's turn," said Julianna. Alexa nodded in response.

Rather than using his terrain, Michael watched on as the orc took down his angel spawn.

"He still didn't use it. What is he waiting for?" a flustered Alexa said.

"Harnessing two terrains to cast orc blitz enchantment," said the witch.

"She's casting a spell?" All four of them said in shock.

"Battling orc can now attack all familiars the opponent controls. Furthermore, one takes no damage this turn," said the witch.

"What?" Michael asked, now taken aback.

"My thoughts exactly. A two terrain enchantment can't be that strong," said Alexa. She took a deep breath. "I'm sure Michael knows that. He was probably hoping to use those angel spawn to stall out until he had more terrain to cast stronger enchantments. This angel is clearly cheating with overpowered enchantments only Lucifer would know."

The orc took down Michael's two remaining angel spawn, leaving his battlefield empty in a fit of growls as Michael shielded his face from the impact.

"What's worse is when creatures exchange blows; the prevailing beast would take battle damage equal to the strength of the fallen beast until the end of the turn. But, that absurd enchantment even prevents that." Alexa's nostrils flared with contempt.

"This is fucking outrageous!" Julianna shouted.

Nearly falling to his knees, Michael panted heavily from the unbridled force of the vicious orc.

"These monsters. They're every bit as real as I remember."

"Don't lose hope, Michael," Isabella said, looking over at him.

"She right. Get off the ground and teach this cheating witch bitch a lesson!" said Alexa.

Cheating? Michael thought. He picked himself up and smiled. *I see now. This test is greater than I thought. Very well.*

"Battle phase concluded. Ending turn," said the witch.

"Then, I guess it's my turn," said Michael. The girls looked at him, taken by surprise at the smile on his face.

"I cast my second light terrain," he said as the sun grew brighter, swallowing a portion of the storm. "And once again, I'll end my turn without harnessing anything."

"I know he has no familiars, but what is he thinking leaving himself wide open again?" Isabella asked.

"That dumbass is going to get killed if he gets attacked by two orcs," said Alexa.

"Maybe he'll make it," Ursula suggested in a hopeful voice.

"Doubtful. The first person knocked out in a battle loses. Unless he can withstand the might of two orcs and whatever else the witch throws his way without breaking the rules, he's finished. I'm just glad this was only a test," said Alexa.

The witch looked over at Michael and nodded. "Commencing turn three. Casting third dark terrain."

The surrounding wasteland grew. The air grew cold with the shadows amassing amidst the competing sunlight.

"Activating orc battle ground enchantment. Doubling forces, once more." Two more orcs emerged from the cave, roaring ferociously at Michael.

"Four orcs? Not good!" Isabella's eyes flared with terror.

"Now casting six angel spawn to opponent's side of the battlefield."

"Four orcs. Just one thing missing," Michael said with a smile as the angel spawn appeared before him.

"Now harnessing all three terrains to perform enchantment, storm the castle," said the witch.

"That can't be good, either," Ursula commented.

"It's not." Alexa flipped through her book. "Michael's certifiably fucked. That enchantment does, well, you'll see."

A massive black dragon broke from the roof of the cave with a thunderous roar and breathed crimson flames all around the sky. Their hearts skipped a beat, enveloped with terror from the dragon's ferocious presence.

"Four orcs and a dragon. This seems familiar, somehow." Said Isabella.

"Then, it sounds like you've heard of the legend of the sapphire woods. A dangerous place known for once harboring legendary beasts like the one you see before you," Julianna said, staring at the army standing before Michael.

"Michael made it a good couple rounds, but in the end, there's only so much one can take on, god or not," said Alexa.

"It's for the best. Angels shouldn't be tampering with demon magic, anyway. Hopefully, he'll sort this once it's over," said Isabella.

"I don't know," Ursula began, "Michael doesn't seem bothered at all. In fact, he seems to be enjoying himself."

Lost in discussion, the rest of the girls looked over at Michael, who continued to smile. It was almost as if he was holding back his laughter.

"There's no way. Does he have a plan to take out four orcs and a dragon?" Alexa exclaimed.

"Dragon's first ability commence. Double orc forces."

"That means"—Ursula lapsed, as did everyone else when four more orcs stampeded out of the caves, roaring and swinging their clubs.

Michael's smile only grew with the army opposing him, unhindered by the presence of a dozen more angel spawn.

"At least his army's growing exponentially." Isabella took a sigh of relief.

"And those new orcs can't attack," Ursula added.

"Dragon's second ability commence."

"A second one?" Julianna shouted.

"Obliterate all angel spawn."

"All of them?" Michael's eyes widened with surprise.

"Trample damage inflicted upon destruction," said the witch.

"You've got to be fucking kidding me!" said Alexa.

The dragon belched a heavy gush of flames upon the angels, scorching them to an ashen pile of powder. The pain of their demise quickly registered on Michael instead, to which he responded with a hateful glare as the fiery jolts surged through his body. Still, he stood his ground, ready for his next move.

Standing his ground as the pain of fiery jolts surged through his body, Michael looked up with a hateful glare in his eyes.

"That face," Julianna began, "Michael's at such a disadvantage, and yet when I look into those eyes, I know there's no way he could lose. But how?"

"I'm almost starting to feel bad for his opponent. Just one look of that murderous stare and you know there's something brewing behind it," said Ursula.

"Even with no familiars ... Michael can still"—she stopped mid-thought, as Michael blocked the attack with his scepter.

"He blocked it?" Ursula said, watching as he pushed the giant beast back. "Is he allowed to do that?"

"Yes You can block up to one direct attack with a weapon per game. Shame it's only one. And yet"—Alexa could not look away at his unbreakable resolve in his eyes.

"Orc two attacks opponent"—

Before she could finish, she noticed the first orc pushing Michael towards the ground while he fought against its strength.

"Unbelievable. That beast must be thirty feet tall, yet he's handling it without breaking a sweat," said Alexa.

"We can't forget he pretty much did the same with your titan. And that creature was way bigger," said Ursula.

Alexa nodded along in a trance, and the rest of the girls did the same. The orc's fist plummeted down onto Michael, primed to crush him. After a moment of silence, Michael rose from the crater his heels dug. With a gritty grunt, he pushed the orc's fist back with a surprisingly minimal effort—almost as if to belittle the strength of the very beasts that once haunted him, as a way of saying he'd be haunted no more.

"He blocked it with his bare hands. No way," said Isabella.

The witch looked down and paused.

"Ending turn."

"That's it? She still has three more orcs to attack with," said Isabella.

"Would you go into battle against an army of one with the capacity to intimidate an orc?" Julianna asked.

Michael looked across with his unbreakable nerve at his opponent. He took a deep breath as he gazed into the beasts before him.

A realization finally hit him. A part of him had known all along since the witch appeared, but now, he fully embraced his theory.

That dream he had in the tavern was no dream, but a vision of the future. A vision foretelling his rivalry with Lucifer. He saw that now. These beasts of his nightmare were merely his first test in defeating Lucifer, and judging by his tactics thus far, Lucifer was not pulling punches. Michael wasn't shaken though. After all, he still had many moves of his own.

"My turn. And I cast my third light terrain," Michael announced. The sun grew even brighter than before, engulfing more of the darkness.

"May this ray of light symbolize my hope for a better

future as I harness all my terrains." He then looked over at the girls.

I'll prove I have what it takes to crush the demon king by crushing this witch android and breaking through Lucifer's first test. I swear, he thought.

"He's finally using his terrains," said Ursula.

"This is it. Someone will lose this turn. I can sense it, somehow," Alexa said, wide-eyed.

"With three terrains, I cast an enchantment known as 'revival of the divine'." An angel spawn descended from the clouds and onto his side of the battlefield as the golden rays cast their light upon it.

"He cast a spawn. But, how?" Alexa said, dumbfounded.

"By waiting until my third turn to harness any terrains, I can perform the spell that will mark the beginning of the end for you."

"What does that enchantment do?" Ursula wondered.

"And how does he know it?" Isabella asked.

"It must be a memory he regained. I can't find anything on this enchantment," Alexa said, flipping through her book. She prepared to move towards her device when she felt a powerful gust of wind.

Michael clenched his fists and looked at the beasts before him. "You were a fool to cast all those spawn because now, they'll be your undoing."

"What's he about to do?" Ursula asked.

"This enchantment allows me to cast any duplicate spawn that's been conjured during this game. Then, I can destroy one creature on the battlefield for every one of your spawn destroyed so far. Lastly, you take trample damage equal to the power of your fallen beast!"

"No way, he's beating Lucifer at his own game," Alexa said, shaking with both fear and excitement. The other girls looked on, nervously.

"You destroyed over twenty spawn during our game. Now, say goodbye to all of your familiars!"

Michael raised his scepter high. As the clouds grew dark and the thunder roared, lightning struck all around them, sending chills of fear through the girls' bodies.

"Did I forget to mention that if you run out of familiars, you take the rest of the damage as damage equal to your own power? It's over!"

"Unholy shit!" the girls exclaimed.

"This is the true extent to not only my power but to my undying loyalty to those I care about too. This world is shit and I couldn't care less about all others who inhabit it, but anyone who crosses my friends pays the price. Goodbye!"

The lightning from his enchantment came crashing down, striking everything opposing his unbridled hatred. First, the orcs, then the dragon, and lastly, the witch. The gruesome assault filled with blood and screams left nothing but their charcoal remains blowing in the unforgiving winds as the light swallowed the last of the darkness.

With his enemies' demise, the storm cleared, and the sun dominated the sky again. Michael fell to his knees, overcome with fatigue. The girls walked over to him in complete shock.

"Michael, where did that come from?" Alexa asked.

Michael took a deep breath as he struggled back up. The four of them helped him to his feet.

"I don't know. I must have read the spell while you were skimming through your books," Michael said.

"Do you think it's possible you just knew the spell before and you happened to regain the memory?" Isabella asked.

Michael's head ached. "It's possible. If that's true, I'll be sure not to forget that spell again."

"You got lucky calling it when you did. I was certain you were finished," said Alexa.

"Thanks," Michael said with a dim eyed glare.

"You know what I meant," said Alexa.

"I do." Michael smiled. "And I think a part of me wanted to remember that spell. Not just to win some game, but to prove to myself I'm above being intimated by my visions and dreams No longer will I see them as nightmares or obstacles, but as opportunities to better myself with the knowledge they could give."

"I think you're reading a lot into this like before with the image of that estate," said Alexa.

"Maybe I am," Michael began, "but I think there's meaning in everything I see. And in the case of my dreams; something to prove."

"And what is it you have to prove?" Alexa asked.

The four of them looked with curiosity as Michael looked to them with a smile. His confidence mystified them as the light from above cast over him.

"That Lucifer is neither going to intimidate me with any of his games nor will he get away with what he's done. Stealing, physical abuse, threatening to enslave this world with his scheme of amassing all the titans... It ends now."

The four of them looked at him and smiled.

"And we'll end it together," said Isabella.

"That, we will." Michael nodded.

He looked towards the heavens with a stoic gaze. He could almost sense the clouds trembling under his resolution.

"Wherever you are, demon king, know that you won't get away with your endeavors. Next time we meet, be it in this reality or my dreams, you'll be the one to lose. So, get ready. Because it's only a matter of time. Until I call checkmate."

FAR FROM WHERE THE FIVE OF THEM CONFIDENTLY STOOD, Lucifer hunched over his desk with a furious gaze.

"Inconceivable. To think the archangel could wield the power of a titan. He'll prove a more formidable foe than I thought."

He sewed the fragments of his broken mask together with thread crafted from his shadows. With the last stitch, the thread melded into the mask. It appeared now just as it was before it shattered.

Shame little Hecate isn't here. I could have used her to sew this. Oh, well. What's getting your hands dirty from time to time?

Lucifer placed the mask onto his face, staring outside his window. The sun was absent out there. In its place, the crimson moon hung supreme.

"None of this will matter in the end because I will return soon enough. Take haven with your friends, traversing whichever dimensions you like. It matters not to me. Any corner of our cosmos, any realm of reality, even in your darkest and most unforgiving dreams, I will find you, Michael. And when we meet again, I will cast you down from your arrogant ways and rule over the omniverse as its sole overlord. Lest you wait, brother. Your chance to cast judgment over this world beside has now imploding like a dying star. Now, it's only a matter of time until the king overcomes the ace."

ABOUT THE AUTHOR

J.J. Egos: is an emerging author of dark fantasy and the writer of the Demonheart series. This is the 2nd installment in that journey.

The concept was birthed from a very bleak and surreal dream I had long ago. Those dreams have been taking form between these pages been ever since.

COME AND LEAVE A REVIEW

I f you enjoyed the book, please leave a review. I love connecting with my readers and want to know what you feel about my story. Plus the more reviews we have, the more readers will find the story.

Writing for you is my dream! Thank you for making it possible.

JOIN MY MAILING LIST

If you'd like to stay informed on all future updates, and be a part of any future giveaways, beside to sign up for my newsletter below. I'll see you there!

HTTPS://DASHBOARD.MAILERLITE.COM/FORMS/333290/
8048480384817672б/SHARE

LOOKING FOR MORE?

You can continue the Demonheart story by picking by the next installment here!

DEMONHEART 3- CULT OF BLACKWATER

DEMONHEART

Book 3

Cult Of Blackwater

J.J. Egosi

.